SAVED

JOAQUIN FUERTES MAFIA CARTEL

FUERTES MAFIA CARTEL

CHIQUITA DENNIE

LATEST RELEASES

Latest Releases from Chiquita Dennie
    The Early Years-A Prequel Short Story
    Antonio and Sabrina: Struck in Love 1, 2, 3,4
    Heart of Stone, Book 1 (Emery & Jackson)
    Heart of Stone Book 1.5 Emery &Jackson A Valentine's
Day Short
    Janice and Carlo: Captivated By His Love
    Heart of Stone, Book 2 (Jordan and Damon)
    Temptation
    Heart of Stone, Book 3 (Angela and Brent)
    Bottoms Up Heart of Stone, Book 3.5 (Jessica and
Joseph Short)
    Cocky Catcher
    Bossy Billionaire
    Love Shorts: A Collection of Short Stories
    Joaquin Fuertes (The Fuertes Cartel Book 1)
    Joaquin Fuertes (The Fuertes Cartel Book 2)
    Exposed (Salvation Society Novel)
    Upcoming Releases (2021):
    She's All I Need

Antonio and Sabrina: Struck in Love 5
Summer Break Series 1-3
Refuel (A Driven World Novel)
Pressure (A Driven World Novel)
Until Serena (HEA World Novel)
Heart of Stone, Book 4 (Jessica and Joseph)
Something Gained
Dare To Love

For my Family

I want to dedicate this book to my family and friends.
You're always with me no matter where I go and everything you've taught me has made me a better person.

AUTHOR INSPIRATION

"Shed the negativity, not your dreams."

—Chiquita Dennie

DISCLAIMER

This work of fiction contains strong language and explicit sexual content and is only intended for mature readers. This story may contain unconventional situations, language, and sexual encounters that may offend some readers. If you're looking for sweet, fluffy romance, I would recommend another book. This book is for mature readers (18+).

INTRODUCTION

Grab some wine and get ready for more spicy, sinful, sexy suspense with Joaquin and Sofia.

Are you signed up for my newsletter?

Join today and find out all the latest in new releases, contests, giveaways, sneak peeks and more.

www.chiquitadennie.com

SYNOPSIS

Joaquin

I never expected things would get this out of control. My sins have come back to haunt me and affect everyone I love. I forced my way into her life and turned things upside down. Not only am I dealing with snakes in business, but her family, and friends think we shouldn't be together. The only problem is that I'll never let her go.

Sofia

It wasn't meant to be like this. I think back to the first time I laid my eyes on Joaquin Fuertes, and thought I could control my feelings and not get caught up with falling in love. Now I'm in a position to never see my family and friends again. I ask myself should I leave my life behind or try to make things work with him? The only problem is that I doubt he'll ever let me go, but do I really want to be away from him anyway?

"I told you already, Joaquin, you don't run my life."

"I'm not trying to run your life, I'm trying to love you," he responded, groaning in frustration. I turned toward the shouting outside and saw multiple cars arrive.

"I love you too; what's the name of your boat?" I watched Leonardo get out of the car and shake hands with a man I'd never seen before. They exchanged words, and he passed Leonardo a black bag.

"It's called Sofia. I had all your favorite foods ordered and clothes picked up, so you don't have to worry about anything."

Leonardo turned, headed toward the car, and opened the passenger seat. I grabbed my purse as he opened the door, then yanked the phone out of my hand. "Leonardo, what are you doing?!" I shouted.

"Bitch, let's go!" he shouted at me angrily and shoved me to a man. "She's all yours!" he spat. I screamed at Leonardo, trying to get out of his hold on my arm. I tried yelling for Joaquin to help me. Leonardo placed his hand over my mouth as I kicked and screamed to get out of his arms. I could hear Joaquin yelling through the phone. "Sofia! Sofia! Leonardo, I swear to God, if you hurt her, your entire bloodline will be extinguished." I heard Joaquin yell.

"Bitch, you bit me," Leonardo yelled, before he slapped me across the face. I fell on the ground in shock and pain as he ripped the back of my dress trying to pull me back.

"No, let me go! Please... Please, I won't tell," I begged, as he handed me off to the other guy.

CHAPTER 1

*J*oaquin

I tried calling Sofia's number again to try and get some type of location of where she could be. I had no clue of who could have done this since my line of work puts me in the line of fire from not only rival cartels, but also, the police in both America and my home country have me on their radar. I try to keep a low profile as Ghost, but if anything happened to Sofia I couldn't promise not to kill off every head of all the cartel families.

"Speed up and get me to the dock now!" I shouted to my driver. Dialing my car phone again it was finally answered.

"Sofia! Sofia!" I yelled and heard an evil laugh.

"Boss, good to hear from you," Leonardo said.

"Where is she?" I questioned.

"She went on a little trip and said for me to tell you not to bother calling again," Leonardo spoke in a menacing yet annoyed tone.

"Do you really want to play with your life, Leonardo?

You know what I'm capable of doing," I stated. Chilled silence lengthened over the phone before I spoke once more. "I suggest you contact your mother and say goodbye now."

"What are you talking about?" Leonardo fearfully asked.

"You'll find out soon," I replied then ended the call as he screamed my name. Loving another person while being in this business was one of the reasons I didn't get involved with women. It only brought out the other side of me that I tried to keep hidden and now Sofia would see the real Joaquin "Ghost" Fuertes because I planned on hunting down everyone that had a hand in hurting her. From the captain of the ship to Leonardo's mother for giving birth to a spineless piece of shit son.

The car finally pulled up at the dock, and I could see the boat was already halfway in the middle of the ocean. I could only hope and pray Sofia was able to stay calm and not get hurt by fighting back. I knew the way these men thought and worked. When I killed Queen it was quick and smooth, no witnesses or anything tying it to the organization. I looked down as my phone started ringing from an unknown number. Normally I wouldn't answer, but something in my gut told me this wasn't an ordinary call. I hit answer while still watching as the boat got farther away.

"Mr. Fuertes." I heard a voice I couldn't recognize come through the phone.

"Who is this?" I asked.

"I have something you want," he stated.

"Joaquin! Help me!" I heard Sofia cry out.

I closed my eyes trying to control my emotions.

"Shush...sweetheart," he told her over the phone, and I heard Sofia whimpering don't touch me.

I felt my heart pumping fast and clenched my fists.

"I know Leonardo helped you," I ground out through clenched teeth. My whole being boiled with fury. My jaw ached from my actions, but my focus, my priority was Sofia.

"I figured it wouldn't take you nothing but a second," he remarked.

"What...do...you...want?" I spoke, my voice low and deadly.

"You took something from me Ghost. It's only fair that I do the same thing to you."

"*Ahhh! Stop please,*" Sofia screamed.

"Since you know my name, it's only right I know yours."

I paced in front of the dock back and forth as Gabriella, Gael, and Hugo pulled in next to my car.

"I think that will be arranged really soon. But in the meantime, I'm going to have a little fun with my guest," he said and hung up abruptly.

"Fuckkkk!!" I shouted, removing my tie to stop the suffocation I was feeling. I knew I wasn't really suffocating, but my rage and anguish were such I felt like I would combust if my tie was on one minute longer. I watched as the boat faded out to sea and my stomach dropped knowing that I'd probably never see her again.

"Joaquin you need to see this," Gael said and stepped next to me holding his phone. I froze, my eyes wide as I struggled to comprehend what I was reading.

Actress, Singer Sofia Chambers Kidnapped-The Daily Blast

Sofia Chambers Worldwide Superstar is Missing-Celebrity Gossip Magazine

"Fuck!"

"Exactly, we need to regroup at your place and call her people," Gael mentioned.

My jaw tightened further at having to call her manager and parents. They would only use this as a means to keep her away from me. Gael tapped me on the shoulder and we walked back to my car and I got inside while Gael slid next to me as Gabriella and Hugo rode in the next car.

"Your father wants to meet tomorrow," Gael stated, and I waved him off.

"I don't have time for him."

"He might be able to help, Joaquin," Gael told me, and I sharply turned my head toward him.

"You think he had something to do with this?" I questioned as the driver drove back to the city.

"I doubt he would stoop to that level," Gael replied, once again scrolling through his phone.

"I wouldn't put anything past anyone," I said as our eyes locked.

"I agree, but you know I've always been loyal."

"Let's hope so," I mumbled to myself.

Thirty minutes later we made it back to my place, jumped out of the car, and walked inside to head toward the elevator. I checked my watch and it was going on ten o'clock. Since the blogs already had the story I could only imagine the major news stations would blast the story soon. Gabriella and Hugo followed us onto the elevator. I stood in the corner with my head angled up and my eyes closed trying to will myself not to go crazy. The elevator dinged and we stepped off. Hugo stopped to pick up a yellow envelope.

"Take Gabriella and check out back to see if you can find anything. This is preposterous that someone was bold enough to leave an envelope in front of my door."

"Stay calm, Joaquin," Gael said.

"Fuck being calm!" I shouted as I stepped in Gael's face.

He held his hands up and took a step back. I could feel

myself slowly slipping into that dark place again. Without Sofia, there was no reason for me to spare a soul on this planet. I opened the envelope and pulled the photos out of Sofia showing her in various scenarios—alone at the studio, entering the recording booth, and out to eat. Some of the photos even had me with her or with my people. I slapped the photos in Gael's hands.

"How was someone able to get these without me knowing?" I forced my key in the door and tossed my jacket on the couch before I headed to the bar and poured a drink.

"I'm starting to think it could be an inside job," Gael said as Gabriella and Hugo walked inside shaking their heads.

"We didn't see anything." Gabriella bit her lip.

"Check the cameras," I said before I gulped down the scotch and poured another glass.

"What do you want me to do about her people? We need to get ahead of this," Gael informed me.

"Call them over first and then we'll see what they think about calling her parents."

Gael stood up and walked out of the living room as he talked on the phone. My gaze lingered on each person in the room as I wondered if they had betrayed me.

"Boss," Gabriella muttered and walked over to the couch and looked at the screen.

My face reddened. "Who is that?" I questioned as I glared at the person wearing all black with their face covered up.

"I think it's Leonardo, just from the body build. No one has access besides him and us," Gabriella stated and rewound the footage of the guy as he stepped into the frame and placed the envelope down without ever showing his face.

"He knew the cameras were there," I spoke.

"Exactly, which means we have a snake in the camp," Gabriella sneered before she cracked her knuckles.

"Cassidy is on her way here now. Edward didn't answer the phone," Gael remarked.

"He didn't answer his phone? The same night Sofia is kidnapped?" My brows drew together.

"Edward's a sleazeball, but I doubt he could pull something like this off on his own," Gael told me.

"Should we call Antonio?" Hugo asked.

"No."

"He's gone through the same thing, Joaquin. Maybe he could help." Gael's eyes burned with frustration.

"The less people involved the better."

"I disagree, we need everyone that can put in calls," Gael replied.

"I said no. I'm Ghost, this can be fixed without more people getting involved."

"Do you hear yourself?" Gael questioned.

"Gael, drop it."

"You're not invisible, Joaquin."

"I fucking know that! I'm Ghost for a reason," I yelled in Portuguese.

"Brother, I just want to help you." Gael jammed his hands in his pockets. The doorbell rang and Hugo opened it slowly and I saw Cassidy standing on the other side.

"Thanks for coming," I spoke as I waved for her to take a seat.

"I had no choice when you said something happened to Sofia," Cassidy remarked, and my chest tightened. I sat down on the chair opposite of Cassidy; my hands clasped together in my lap.

"Sofia's been kidnapped," I muttered.

"What! OMG...I need to call the police." Cassidy jumped

up out of her seat and I motioned for Gabriella to take her phone.

"What are you doing!" Cassidy screamed.

I watched as Gabriella tossed Cassidy's phone in her pocket.

"Cassidy, we can't get the police involved."

"Are you crazy? The police should have been called the second you found out," Cassidy grumbled, holding her hand out for her phone.

"Cassidy, my work is not the most conventional," I said.

"I know you're a gangster or something," Cassidy mumbled.

"Something like that, but Sofia has always been protected."

"Until today," Cassidy spat.

"Yes and the reason being is because someone wants my attention and they decided to get me back by taking Sofia," I informed her, and stood up, grabbed my glass and refilled it.

"You need a clear mind, Joaquin," Gael said, pointing toward the glass.

"This is the only thing keeping me sane," I stated, and went back to the couch.

"Hugo, go back to the dock with some men and see if anything was left behind, maybe Sofia fought with them." Gael crossed his arms over his chest.

I stood up and walked to the bedroom to change my clothes. I turned and saw one of my shirts on the bed and lifted it up and smelled it remembering this was Sofia's favorite shirt whenever she came over and spent the night.

"I knew you thugs would hurt Sofia in some way!" I heard a gasp and yelling back and forth. I ran back into the living room and saw Gabriella choking Edward as Hugo and Gael tried to separate them.

"Let him go," I said as I dropped the shirt on the back of the couch. He bent over trying to catch his breath as Gabriella glared at him.

"She's an animal," Edward spat.

"I see you got our message."

"Where is Sofia? I don't think this is a kidnapping plot." He straightened his jacket and tie.

"She's been taken and before you start, I'll cut your fucking tongue out if you say anything else besides *How can I help?*" I demanded.

Edward glanced over at Cassidy then back to me with a grave expression.

"I don't understand why we can't call the police," Cassidy spoke.

"Because the police will only make things worse," Gael responded as he focused his eyes on Edward.

"What can we help with?" Edward mumbled.

"Two gossip magazines or whatever you call them have posted about Sofia's kidnapping. I want them shut down and for you to find out who did it."

"We can try, but most times they'll say an anonymous source," Cassidy explained, raising her arms wide.

"Take Gabriella with you," I stated and both their eyes darted over to Gabriella checking the bullets in her gun.

"You have any idea who did this?" Edward questioned.

"An enemy. I can promise that once I find out who, they'll wish they were never born," I said.

"I'll help, but just know the second we find Sofia, I'll do everything I can in my power to convince her to stop dating you. If you truly love her, I suggest you leave her alone," Edward responded, before he turned to yank the door open and walked out. Cassidy and Gabriella strolled behind him. I lifted the bottle of scotch to refill my glass and Gael grabbed it out of my hand.

"Get your head out of the bottle. We need you clear and focused," Gael said, placing the top back on and I nodded in agreement. We both stayed silent for a few minutes until Hugo spoke.

"What about her apartment?" Hugo asked.

"Take Alex with you and report back to me," I said and grabbed my jacket off the floor not even thinking to change clothes.

"Where are you going, Joaquin?" Gael asked.

"I need to talk with Antonio." I swiped my keys off of the table.

"I'm going with you," Gael insisted.

Hugo, Gael, and I left my apartment and went our separate ways, leaving through the back alley. I jumped into the driver's side of my Ferrari and Gael went to the passenger side. I stuck the key in the ignition and headed out, not waiting for him to slide the seat belt on.

CHAPTER 2

Sofia
That same night.

I was sitting inside of the room on the bed, looking out the window as he talked to one of his men. I tried my best to fight and jump off the boat, but he locked me inside of the bedroom. I was beyond terrified of what he was planning on doing and where he was taking me, and I still had no clue who he was or what he wanted with me. I saw them stop talking and he came back down to the lower deck and I heard the lock turn before he stepped inside.

"Please let me go," I said as I wiped the tears from my cheek.

"You're really a fabulous actress, Miss Chambers. Bravo," he replied and grinned.

I scooted back further as he stepped further into the room. One of his men stood behind him with a gun.

"I have some food for you."

"I'm not hungry," I responded.

"Do you want to go home? See your family and Joaquin?" he asked.

I nodded yes before verbally responding, "I do."

"Then follow my instructions," he replied then turned to walk out.

"Then I can go home?" I asked as I followed behind.

"Maybe," he answered and sat down at the table and picked up the napkin, placing it on his lap. He had a candlelight dinner with two plates that held steamed vegetables, baked salmon, oysters, and pasta with cut up lobster.

"Why are you doing this?" I questioned, lowered down in the chair.

"He took something from me."

"Who?" I inquired.

"Ghost," he spat, with a hard grimace.

"Who's Ghost?" I inquired.

"You have no clue, do you?"

"No dammit and I want to get out of here!" I shouted, and tried to stand up. The man with the gun pushed me back in the seat.

He flicked his hand and the guy with the gun nodded and walked out of the room.

"Joaquin *Ghost* Fuertes is a dangerous man, Sofia."

A chill went down my spine.

"Who are you?" I asked.

He smirked.

"Ciro Vitale," he responded as he reached his hand out for me to shake.

"Why are you doing this to me?"

"Joaquin killed my niece, Queen Vitale," he replied.

"That has nothing to do with me," I said.

"It has everything to do with you, because Ghost decided to kill the daughter of a Cartel Boss," Ciro spoke.

"I don't know anything about that."

"Eat, we can finish our talk tomorrow," Ciro stated.

"Are you going to kill me?" I queried, gripping the knife beside me. His eyes darted to my hand and smirked.

"I wouldn't do anything stupid if I were you. A lot of sharks in these waters," he responded as he cut into his meal.

"I can pay you. Please, I have money, if I go missing a lot of people will worry."

"That's what I plan on," he said, sneering.

"If Joaquin or Ghost is the person you say is so crazy to kill the daughter of a mobster what do you think he will do if something happens to me?"

"While he's distracted by you missing? A few friends of mine will take what's owed to them," Ciro explained. I jumped up, raised the knife under his chin and he grinned as I glared at him.

"Have your men turn around and take me back."

"Don't worry, Sofia, we're not leaving the country," Ciro said as he grasped my wrist, twisted it around and almost broke it making me drop the knife as I screamed.

"You little bitch!" Ciro yelled.

"Please, let me go," I cried out.

"I should punish you for that move, but I won't this time. I have plans for Joaquin and they include you."

"Ciro turn on the news." His henchman marched inside, picked up the remote and turned on the tv.

"*We have some reports that Sofia Chambers is missing,*" the Channel 5 news anchor announced.

"*That's right, Elizabeth, so far we have Celebrity Gossip magazine reporting. We still have not confirmed,*" Jonathan, the second news anchor reporter, replied.

"Good," Ciro said.

"Good! I'm all over the news and probably social media. I demand to be sent home," I shouted, and he backhanded me.

"Take her to the bedroom," Ciro said.

"No, let me go. Get your fucking hands-" He pointed the gun in my face.

"My men will treat you with respect on my orders or they can treat you like the whore that you are, Miss Chambers," Ciro seethed as he sparked up the cigar he'd taken out of his pocket.

"Move," his man said and pushed me forward to the bedroom.

"Can I get the food?" I asked, hearing my stomach growling.

"No," the guy blurted out with a raspy voice.

I crawled on top of the bed and curled my legs up to my chest, and cried to myself as I felt the boat stop. All of a sudden I heard gunfire and yelling from up top.

"Go grab her now!" Ciro shouted.

Pop! Pop!

"OMG!" I screamed as the bullets went back and forth, hitting the window of the room I was in. The door burst open and two of his men came in and dragged me out.

"Let me go."

"Hurry up," yelled the shorter guy wearing a military vest, dark boots, and a patch over his eye.

"She's acting like a bitch," the taller one stated as he gripped my arm tighter and pulled me out of bed.

"I can walk," I said, stumbling to get up right.

Finally, he let me go and shoved me to keep me walking forward.

The shorter man with the hard glare, soulless eyes from out on the lower deck, stood talking with another gunman. I could hear Ciro on top barking orders. Gunfire was still going off as I looked out further and saw a smaller boat. I squinted my eyes, but it was hard to tell who was on the other boat and if they were here to save me.

"Take her to the boat," Ciro commanded as he continued firing shots. I was still wearing my dress and heels without a jacket, but I'd rather die trying to get away than stay with these men. We continued down the right side of the boat and I saw another one with a gun holding a guy and wearing a life vest.

"Get in," the guy with the eye patch told me.

I looked down then up into his eyes and behind me. Thinking this was my only chance, I decided to shove him away and run further to the edge of the back of the boat near the engine and I jumped off as I felt the sting from a bullet then the cold freezing temperatures of the sea as I plunged beneath the water.

"Ahhh!!" I felt a sense of relief as my eyes slowly narrowed. I thought I saw a light shining, and a part of me was trying to will myself to start swimming. The wound in my side was something I'd never felt before and all of a sudden, I drifted off as the currents pulled me below.

...

One day later.

I felt whispering around me and heard crying. It sounded like my mom and dad, but they were back home. I wanted to wake up, but my body was weighing heavy, like something was sitting on my chest. I prayed that wherever I was, it was away from those men and they'd never find me again. The way Ciro spat Joaquin's name and how he killed his niece, and having that burden of wanting to save myself and warn him was too much to bear. Hearing gunshots over and over again and the cold icy water where I almost drowned caused my body to heat up again.

"Doctor, is she all right?" I heard a voice say.

All of a sudden the beeping noises became elevated.

"Sofia, we need you to calm down."

My eyes felt like they were moving at a rapid pace.

"Let me go!" I screamed.

"Sofia, you're safe, sweetie."

"No, he's going to kill me," I yelled.

A soft gentle voice said, "Doctor do something."

"Nurse, give her a sedative to calm her down. Let her get some rest," the doctor spoke and I drifted back into that dark place. Eased into a deep sleep, like a movie replaying, I watched myself in slow motion jumping into the water and felt the sting of the bullet hit me.

Two days later I slowly opened my eyes and glanced around the room. I lifted my hand to check my side still feeling the pain from the gunshot. The room was white, more than likely I'm in the hospital and still in America since the tv was running an entertainment show about me.

"Where am I?" I questioned. My mom jumped up and came to my bedside, caressed my cheek.

"You're awake, thank God."

"Where am I?" I asked again.

"You're in the hospital, baby. Your father and I have been here every day," Mom said.

"How long have I been sleeping?"

"Three days," Mom replied.

She picked up the jug of water and poured some in a cup.

"Here drink this," she said.

"Mmmm...thanks," I said and gave her the cup back to place on the food tray.

"We thought we lost you for a moment," Mom said as she kissed my cheek.

"What did the doctor say and where is Dad?"

"The doctor is checking your test results and Dad went to the cafeteria for food."

"How did you find me?"

The second I spoke those words the door opened, and I smelled that same cologne that had taken over my mind and body since the first time we met at Antonio's.

"I was hoping you'd be awake," Joaquin stated as he stalked to the edge of the bed. He ran a hand across my foot. He didn't look like the clean cut Joaquin I was used to being around in suits and all clean shaven. Instead, he stood before me, slightly disheveled with a beard and mustache.

"What happened to me?" I questioned him and he darted his eyes toward my mother.

"We can talk about that later," Joaquin stated.

"No, I want to talk about it now!" I demanded, and the heart monitor started beeping.

"Sofia, relax, baby. Your blood pressure will go up and they'll put you back to sleep," Mom explained.

"I need to talk to Joaquin, can you give us a minute?" I looked up, and she nodded in answer.

She went over to pick up her purse and walked out of the room as Gael held the door open. Joaquin's entire demeanor was off and I felt somewhere in my gut that he was lying and probably hiding more secrets. I was very aware of who he was when I agreed to go out with him, but he promised to keep me protected and now I was sitting in a hospital bed with a gunshot wound and three days missing from my life.

"I need to know everything that happened," I said.

"Sofia, you're safe. That's what matters," he replied in his thick accent.

"Gael, can you leave us alone please?" I continued glaring at Joaquin as Gael stared between us.

"I'll be right outside," Gael said and turned to walk out. Joaquin came around from the end of the bed to the top and bent down to kiss me on the lips and I moved my head out of the way.

"Don't do this," Joaquin said.

"You need to explain to me how I ended up getting kidnapped by some maniac and then woke up here in a hospital bed."

"Did he touch you?" Joaquin questioned, trying to change the subject.

I felt myself starting to get frustrated and heated. I drew the covers close to my neck and laid my head back on the pillow and closed my eyes for a moment to recall the events on the boat.

"Tell me what's going on, Joaquin. If you want this to work." I pointed between us and his brows narrowed in slits.

"If!" he arrogantly chuckled.

"I just want the truth," I spat, pushed his hands off my leg. He sighed and bobbed his head up and down, grasped my hand and sat on the corner of the bed and stared into my eyes.

"Are you going to sit there and stare at me or tell me the truth?"

The way his eyes bore into me I felt something was missing. He knew more than he was willing to tell me and in a weird way it was probably best that I didn't know anything for my own protection. But if I decided to continue dating him, then all of our cards needed to be on the table.

CHAPTER 3

*J*oaquin
Three days prior.

I RAN the red light not caring if the police saw me driving down the road at a high rate of speed. I needed to find Sofia and that all depended on what Antonio could tell me. I gripped the steering wheel even tighter as I blew through the yellow light causing a car to honk at me.

"Joaquin, slow down, you won't be any help to Sofia if we're dead," Gael grumbled and I pushed the gas even harder, swerving away from a truck that almost hit the right passenger side at the next light. Ten minutes later we pulled up in front of Antonio's restaurant, and jumped out, headed inside pushing the valet and security out of the way and went to the back of the lounge and got on the elevator toward the basement. I walked up to the guard and he nodded before he opened the door for us. Walking in, I saw Antonio, Bruno, and Carlo sitting together talking.

"I expected you half an hour ago," Antonio stated as he leaned over the conference table.

"Who the fuck took her?" I spat, throwing a chair into the wall.

"Has he been like this all night?" Carlo asked, and Gael motioned with his hands out that he wasn't answering that question.

"I know how you feel," Antonio said, and marched around the table to extend his hand out to me.

"I want everything you have on who took her."

"Right now the word is that Ciro Vitale planned this," Bruno told me.

My eyes bugged out in shock.

"He's alive?" I questioned.

"Looks like it and we can't touch him. After killing Queen our hands are tied," Carlo explained.

"You can't kill him, but I will."

"No, Ghost, you've been in the media too much lately," Antonio informed me.

"That's bullshit!" I snapped before I started to punch the wall, only Gael stopped me.

I jerked out of his hold.

"Queen was my call and I take responsibility for that. We need to think about our next steps," Antonio said.

"The bitch deserved to die. Ciro should be next to her."

"Which is why you can't touch him. We have a team preparing to go get Sofia," Carlo said.

"So you have eyes on them?" I asked, getting pissed the longer we stayed there.

"The minute we got word Ciro came into town we had eyes on him," Bruno said.

"No one thought to tell me?"

"Joaquin, you're a hot head like me. The chance of Ciro

surviving one day with you around was not something we could take a chance on," Antonio stated.

"He's not only looking to get revenge on Queen's murder, but we haven't figured out what else he's here for," Carlo said as he pushed a folder down the table toward me. I leaned over and picked it up, then flipped through documents and photos of Ciro talking with Leonardo and Edward.

"I'm going to kill him!" I shouted as I started to leave the room only to be stopped.

"Joaquin calm down," Carlo said.

"I swear to God if you don't let me go, Gael, I'll kill you right now."

"What's in the folder?" Gael asked, and I shoved it in his hands. I ran both palms down my face. All this time I underestimated Edward and thought he wasn't a threat and all along he was playing me.

"That's her manager," Gael spoke up.

"Which makes things even more complicated," Antonio said.

"People go missing all the time."

"Joaquin, we know you're ready to suit up, but you need to listen," Antonio said.

"Explain to me why I shouldn't walk out of here and kill them both?"

"Because Edward and Sofia are both high profile; it's already bad enough that she's been kidnapped," Carlo stated.

"Ciro is looking to take you down and he's started with Alba Industries and working his way with taking Sofia on top of that," Bruno said.

"Does my father know about this?"

"Not yet," Antonio said.

"Where are they now?" Gael asked.

"He's still on the water moving toward Long Island. Ciro's not getting out of the country," Antonio explained.

"How many men are on standby?"

"We have two boats with guys locked and loaded, you can come, but you need to stay on land," Carlo said.

"I need to be there when she gets off the boat."

Antonio shook his head.

"That would only cause Ciro to retreat and kill her. If we go in the dark and take them by surprise, we have a better chance of getting Sofia home safe," Antonio stated.

"What if this was Sabrina?" I snarled. My control was nearly gone and despite knowing what they all were saying was the right thing, I needed to be there, do something. Do damage and seek vengeance upon the man who thought it'd be wise to touch my woman.

"I wasn't there when she was kidnapped in Italy. Sonny found her and sent word," Antonio explained.

"Be smart about this, Ghost, we know she's important to you," Bruno remarked.

"She's the reason my heart even beats."

The door opened and one of his men motioned with a wave of his hand to speak with him. "Go ahead, Sonny, you can speak freely," Antonio stated as he went to the cage in the corner of the basement, typed in a code and grabbed two guns.

"The men are set up and ready to go on your word. We have the front of the dock covered," Sonny explained.

"Sonny, ride with me, Gael, and Joaquin. Carlo you go with Hugo and Bruno in the other car," Antonio said as he offered me a gun.

"I have that covered."

"Joaquin if things don't-" Antonio started to say and I held my hand up to stop him.

"She's coming home," I responded before I marched out

of the room with my team behind me and headed back up the stairs to the top and out to the back entry and loaded up in the black SUV. Mere seconds later, Antonio and Gael climbed in and gave directions to Sonny of where to go. He drove down the street and onto the freeway. My phone vibrated with a picture of Sofia in a bedroom banging on the door.

Unknown: Keep this photo as a reminder.

Me: Ciro I suggest you remember who you're dealing with.

Ciro: Do You remember?Did you give my niece the same respect?

Me: Test me and see what happens.

The car stopped in the parking lot of the loading dock and we filed out and stalked over to the grassy knoll. Antonio had more men wearing life jackets and two speed boats ready to go. I checked my watch; it was going on midnight and I still hadn't heard form Cassidy or Edward.

"You ready?" Antonio asked as he passed me a bullet-proof vest.

"I thought you wanted only two people in the boat," I replied.

"If this was Sabrina, I would do the same, just be careful," Antonio said, then waved for his men to start up the engines. I ran to the edge and hopped inside sliding on the vest, grabbing my gun from behind my back. Gael jumped in the other boat as Hugo and Gabriella got back in the car and rode to the other side of the dark woods. It was getting chillier as the night went on. I could see my breath in the air. Antonio stayed at the dock and directed his men as Sonny drove us out to the spot where he had located Ciro's boat. I thought about hearing Sofia's voice again and worried that if he touched her in any way that would cause her to close herself off. I'd never prayed for anything in the world or cared to even think God listened to me after the things I'd done. Right now looking up to the sky at the full moon and stars I closed my eyes and wished to get her back safe in my arms. A tap on my shoulder brought me out of my thoughts. The bright lights flickered in our direction.

"Get more lights!" the guy that shot at us yelled.

I looked back at Gael as he pointed to the left at the boat that was about a few minutes away from us. We heard some commotion and yelling.

"What's the plan?" Gael asked and I lifted my gun, lined it up and took the safety off right as a gunshot was sent at our boat.

"Focus the light!" the guy that shot at us shouted again.

All three of us ducked as more shots went over our heads. I lifted my gun and sent shots off from my Glock nine. I heard someone scream out in pain.

Pop! Pop! Pop!

"Joaquin, look at the left side," Gael yelled out.

My eyes narrowed as I saw Sofia being pushed from behind and I didn't know what they were planning to do.

"Sonny, head to the other side," I commanded, removing my vest and jacket, preparing to swim over if needed.

The boat picked up speed and took off in her direction while we continued shooting back at the boat. What I wasn't expecting was for Sofia to jump in the water to try and get free.

"Fuck!" I shouted before I jumped in the water and swam to catch her. Not knowing if she survived the gunshot, I was prepared to wipe the entire Vitale family line out.

"Sofia...baby, listen to me," I said as I grabbed her around the waist right when Ciro saw us and started shooting at us in the water.

"Mmmm...help me." Sofia choked on the water.

"Baby, hold on," I said and shoved her back under the water and tried to glide her away from the bullets. Her body went limp in my arms until we got a little more distance away, and finally came up for air two minutes later. I saw Sonny and Gael approach and I lifted Sofia into the boat first.

"Ughhh....don't hurt me," Sofia muttered, trying to fight Gael.

I climbed out of the water and got on the boat and took Sofia out of Gael's arms then placed my jacket over her body to warm her up.

"It's me, baby, Joaquin. You're safe," I repeatedly said, while I rubbed her arms up and down to continue giving her warmth.

"We need to get out of here," Gael responded, and gave me his jacket to put on Sofia.

"Joaquin...Joaquin..." Sofia's eyes rolled to the back of her head as her mouth fell open. She had apparently gone into shock, either due to the gunshot wound or the chill of the water. Regardless, time was of the essence; I refused to lose the woman who owned me, mind, body and soul.

"Faster, God damn it!" I demanded as I tried to give Sofia mouth to mouth. It felt like a lifetime, but only a few seconds before she spit up more water. The boat made it back to land and I picked her up and walked off to the truck that Hugo and Gabriella were in.

"Keep me updated. We have a lot to discuss," Antonio said before he slid the window of the SUV up and drove off. I had Hugo drive to the nearest hospital as I cradled her in my arms. Thirty minutes later we made it to the emergency area, and I got out yelling in order to get some help.

"I need a doctor!"

"Sir, what's the emergency?" a nurse asked as she motioned for a gurney.

"She was in the water a long time and she was shot."

"You stay here and let us take it from here," the short blonde, gray-eyed nurse stated, and I refused, trying to walk behind them, wanting to be with her when she woke up.

"Sir, we need you to fill out some information. Is she your wife?" I looked down at her badge.

"Naomi, she's more than my wife. If anything happens to her," I started to say, and she somberly smiled.

"I understand, sir. Please let us do our jobs and we'll update you soon," Naomi insisted. I nodded and sat down in the waiting area. Gael, Gabriella, and Hugo came in and stood around guarding the front and back entrance.

"Ciro got away," Gael said as he slid his hands in his pockets.

"I want him dead, Gael."

"I understand, brother, but we have to think about our next steps. Your picture and Sofia's are all over the news."

"Fuck the news," I screeched then stood up and kicked the chair away from me, trying to control my temper.

"Your father called and so did your sister," Gael informed me.

"My phone fell in the water."

"Okay, I'll get Alex to get you a new one," Gael said. As he picked the chair up and put it back, the security guard came over with a grimace on his face. If he thought he could intimidate or kick me out, he had another thing coming. People came in and out of the emergency room all night while we waited. Finally, I saw Cassidy run in as the doctor came out to talk to me.

"You brought in the young lady from the water?" the doctor asked as he extended his hand for a shake.

"Sofia Chambers," I said, and his eyes got big.

"We should probably put her in a secluded area away from any prying eyes."

"Does that mean she's alive?" I questioned, holding my breath.

"She is, but we had to perform emergency surgery to get the bullet out, plus being in the water for so long exacerbated the situation."

"What does that mean?" I wondered.

"She's sleeping right now, we didn't want to wake her too early," Doctor Johnson told me.

"How long will she be asleep?" Cassidy asked.

"It's up to her, but if she doesn't wake on her own once the anesthesia wears off, it might end up being a few days. Her body suffered a trauma so right now, rest is important in the healing process."

"Where is she?" Cassidy questioned, hugging herself.

"She's in recovery right now, but we'll move her in a little while to a VIP area," Doctor Johnson informed us as Cassidy and I sat back down in the chairs to wait.

CHAPTER 4

Sofia & Joaquin
Sofia

"So, you've been at the hospital since they first brought me here?" I asked as the nurse came in, smiled at me and started to check my vitals.

"I went home to change clothes after your parents got here on the second day. I left my men here for your protection."

"How are you feeling, Sofia?" Naomi asked as she started the blood pressure machine.

"Exhausted, but hungry," I replied.

"Food will be delivered soon, I just want to make sure you're not having any residual issues," Naomi explained, writing on the chart.

"When can she go home?" Joaquin asked.

"That's up to the doctor, but if everything is looking good, either later today or tomorrow," Naomi stated as she pushed back the cover to check my bandages.

"Does it still hurt? Do you need any extra pain medicine?" Naomi lifted the white bandages and tossed them in the trash.

"A little, but not as much as a few days ago. Will it leave a scar?" I questioned.

Naomi walked over to the door and grabbed what she needed to clean the surgical site.

"A little scar, but nothing to worry about," Naomi said.

I heard a knock on the door as Cassidy stepped in with balloons and a teddy bear.

"I saw your parents outside, and they said I could come up. Am I interrupting?" Cassidy inquired.

"No, you can come in and tell me what's been going on. I'm still trying to process everything," I said.

"Did you tell her?" Cassidy asked.

"Yeah," Joaquin replied.

"Have they caught the guy?" I questioned.

"No, but we have people working on finding him."

"Joaquin, you promised me," I said as I leaned back against the pillow.

"Try not to get upset, dear. I'll bring your food in a few minutes," Naomi told me before she strolled back out. Cassidy sat the balloons on the couch with the teddy bear and handed me the card.

"Edward isn't taking my calls. I'm doing my best to get the blogs under control," Cassidy said.

"Are they camped outside?" I questioned.

"They are and of course they knew me, so they tried to follow me," Cassidy fussed as she rolled her eyes then sat down on the chair next to my bed.

"Put out a statement saying I'm thankful for all of their prayers and well wishes. Keep it simple, but don't feed into anything," I stated. I watched as Cassidy pulled out her phone and started typing up a note.

"You sure that's needed right now? The added stress is probably not good for your recovery," Joaquin advised.

"The stress started with you and look where I ended up!" I fussed, causing the monitor to spike.

"I understand, sweetheart, but I'm working on fixing it so you'll never experience this again."

"How are you going to fix it, huh? Go out and kill everyone that had a hand in this?" I sneered as I motioned around the room I was currently ensconced in.

Before Joaquin could answer, my mother and father peeked through the door. I smiled and waved them inside.

"She's awake, Leroy," my mom, Latonya said, bending down to hug me and kiss my cheek.

"Baby, you scared us to death," my dad, Leroy, stated as he pressed a kiss on my forehead. They were both in the middle age range, around their late fifties or sixties. But they looked far younger, which I was thankful for as I had inherited their genes.

"I'm sorry you guys had to deal with this." Naomi pushed a food tray in and my mother took the top off and helped to get things organized for me to eat.

"We can talk about that later. The most important thing is you're safe," Mom said.

"When can she come home?" Dad asked Naomi.

"The doctor is checking her chart, most likely later today or tomorrow if everything is clear," Naomi informed him.

"Once the doctor clears you, Sofia, we should talk about you coming back home," Mom blurted out.

"That's not happening," Joaquin said and the room went quiet.

"Excuse me?" Latonya responded.

"Joaquin don't start," I said as I cut into my salad.

"My daughter needs rest and to be away from you," Latonya demanded.

"No offense, but Sofia needs to be with me for her own protection."

"We know what you're into, it only takes one phone call to the police," Latonya spat.

"Okay, enough, Ma, I'm not leaving New York. I refuse to be chased away," I explained.

"Sofia, I sent out the press release. I know they'll be calling for you to do an interview soon," Cassidy stated.

"I know and once I talk with the lawyer about the case we can plan out the details," I replied.

"You can't talk with your lawyer, sweetheart."

"What do you mean?" I queried, biting into my burger then taking a sip of water.

"It's complicated and we need to keep it out of police hands."

"Joaquin, you are not making sense."

"We'll discuss this when I get you home," he advised. He stood up to leave and leaned down to kiss me, but I turned my head, unwilling to allow that contact with the current state of affairs so up in the air. I didn't understand why he wouldn't allow the police to get involved; I'd been kidnapped then shot!

"I'll be back."

"Yeah," I mumbled as he walked out leaving my parents and Cassidy in the room.

Joaquin

. . .

GAEL WAS on the phone arguing and I headed in his direction as Gabriella and Hugo pulled away from the door of Sofia's room where they had been standing guard.

"Hugo, I want you to stay here. I have some business to handle."

"Sure boss," Hugo replied.

"Where to now?" Gabriella asked as we stepped out of the hospital and headed to the car.

"Did you get that package for me?" I turned to her as we stopped at the car door.

"Nicely packaged for you," Gabriella commented, and I nodded and opened the door of the passenger side.

"That was your father, it's all the news in Italy about Ciro and Maricio said the next shipment they want to double up," Gael told me. I wasn't too excited to add more product and strain on my men so early.

"Manage it for now and keep an eye out. He's operating under Laurent's orders."

"If something goes wrong," Gael stated as he looked up making eye contact in the rearview mirror.

"His death will be on Laurent's hands."

Gael passed me a phone and I scrolled to see all of my numbers set up and a message from Antonio.

Antonio: We have Ciro coming out of the Westin Hotel.

Me: Keep your men on him.

Antonio: He's trying to do business with Russia.

Me: Fuck doing business, put the word out.

Antonio: How is she doing?

Me: She woke up today and we talked.

Antonio: She knows everything?

Me: I explained how we found her and Edward.

Antonio: He's still MIA?

Me: Yeah, that motherfucker hasn't returned one call.

Antonio: You need me to locate him?

Me: I got my tech people looking into him.

...

Forty minutes later we pulled in front of the warehouse that was out in the middle of nowhere. No interruption would stop me from doing what needed to be done. I looked down at my phone and checked the time. I knew the doctor would probably discharge her by tomorrow, and I wanted to be the one to bring her home so we could talk about everything. I shut the car door and as I got out, Gabriella passed me a gun.

"I won't need that just yet." I handed the gun back to her and removed my jacket and rolled up the sleeves of my white shirt. Usually we handled the torturing together or I let her have free reign, but today I would take pleasure in killing the bastard that thought he could get away with hurting my Sofia.

I looked around the area, the sun was shining, birds chirping. It was more peaceful now than being out in the murky water trying to save my baby's life.

"Arghh ..." she screamed as they saw me walk inside with not one ounce of remorse. I never wanted to stoop to this level, but he left me no choice and today he'd have to watch as I killed his mother in front of him.

"Joaquin, please man. I fucked up," Leonardo said, his face whitening in the chair next to his mother.

"Shut up!" Gabriella shouted as she punched him in the face.

He was picked up by Gabriella two days ago trying to board a plane with his mother. I guess he thought I would spare her, but once you stepped over that line and deliberately tried to hurt the one thing that mattered to me most, then Ghost would come out.

"Shush... save the tears. I mean Sofia had tears when you were sending her off to Ciro right?" I asked, bent down to stare into his eyes. Snot and blood were mixed in with his tears.

"I promise, it wasn't like that. He forced me to do that," Leonardo pleaded.

"Really? Because from what I heard on the phone you took joy in smacking my woman around."

I snapped my finger and Gabriella lifted the knife off the table. I would make his mother suffer a death by torture like I planned on doing with her son. I grabbed it out of her hands and smiled at her.

"I hate that things have to be like this," I said as tears poured out of Leonardo's mother's eyes.

"Ughhh... ahhh..." She tried to move, but we had her arms and legs tied up and a towel inside her mouth.

"Please, Joaquin, I can help you, man...Don't do this," Leonardo begged as I placed the knife under her chin.

"The world we live in states that mothers and children are off-limits, but the minute my woman was taken I didn't exist in this world anymore," I spoke and gripped her hair tight, pulling it back as they both continued to cry and beg.

"Ciro is working with someone close to Sofia," Leonardo yelled out.

I slowly slit her throat as her eyes widened in shock. Leonardo screamed and cried for his mother.

"Tell me something I don't know...Huh...you piece of shit." I stabbed him in the knee and punched him in the stomach.

"Ahhhh!!! Fuckkkk...please don't kill me," Leonardo cried out as I whistled, and my pit bull came running out of the back corner he was chained up against.

"Sit," I commanded.

"Too late, Leonardo. If I were you I would close my

eyes and pray God forgives you, because I don't give second chances," I told him and stabbed him in the left eye.

"Eat." Alessandra went for Leonardo's neck and continued feeding off of him as I stood to clean the knife off with the towel on the table.

"When did you name your dog after your sister?" Gael asked.

I chuckled.

"She's just like my sister, spoiled and angry unless she gets her way."

"That's true," Gael answered as he looked off in thought. I shook off his comment and removed my bloody shirt and tossed it to Gabriella to dispose of as we left the warehouse to head back to the city.

"Who were you arguing on the phone with at the hospital earlier?"

"Nobody," Gael said as he reversed out of the parking lot then headed toward the city.

Gael had never made me not trust him, but lately he'd taken calls more and more that weren't about business, well at least he said they weren't. Every time I tried to talk to him about any problems he blew me off. I'd really hate to have to kill my best friend for working with my enemies.

"If you say so."

He glanced back at me as he drove, and I never lost eye contact. Everybody around me must have felt I went soft with Sofia around me. She'd only made me stronger and I'd prove to everybody not to underestimate why they called me Ghost.

"Burn the building down tonight," I said, and he nodded in answer.

"I need a house out of the city for me and Sofia."

"What about her parents?"

"They'll jump on board in time." I relaxed in the seat.

"Do you think she's ready for that?"

"It's for her safety. Contact the realtor and find something gated." I closed my eyes as we drove back to the hospital to check on Sofia.

CHAPTER 5

Sofia

"You should mind your manners, Sofia," he said as he reached out and gripped my arm.

"Let me go," I shouted. I attempted to bite his hand when he covered my mouth.

"Bitch!" he shouted and smacked me across the face. I fell to the floor and raised my hand to my sore cheek as tears pooled into my eyes.

"I see what Joaquin likes about you." He bent down and grabbed my chin then squeezed.

"He's going to kill you," I muttered as he pushed me down on the floor, pulled out a switchblade and traced it across my cheek down to the top of my dress.

I vainly tried to push his hands away.

"Then, I should make my time worthwhile."

"Get the fuck off me, you bastard," I screamed as I kicked my legs to force him up off me.

"My men wanted to take you for themselves; I said you shouldn't be touched. Are you going to make me change my mind?"

He stood up and placed the blade back in his pocket.

"Joaquin will kill you if anyone touches me."

He smiled and walked toward the door. I pulled myself up from the floor and watched as his henchman came to the door, and they whispered back and forth.

"Would you like something to eat, Sofia?" he asked.

"I want out of here now."

"That's not going to happen. I suggest we become acquainted with each other since you'll be here for a while." He smirked as the door closed behind him.

I ran to the desk drawer to look for anything that could help me get out of here. The entire room only held a bed, tv, and boarded-up windows with bars. Why was this happening to me? I cried and cupped my face, sat down on the bed and was thinking of my family when the door opened again, and two of his men walked in with their guns.

"Get away from me!" I screamed.

Ring! Ring!

"Shit!" Sweat beads ran down my face, and my heart was racing fast from a nightmare of being held captive on a boat. I glanced around my room as I calmed my breathing.

Ring! Ring!

I picked up my cell phone.

"Hello," I said groggily.

"Are you all right?" Joaquin asked.

I checked the time, and it said two am. I'd never had nightmares growing up, but this felt so real.

"It's two am, Joaquin," I responded, wondering why he was calling so late.

"I couldn't sleep," he said.

"That makes two of us."

"You want me to come over?"

"No."

"Baby."

"I promise I'm fine, just a little nightmare."

"I'm coming over," Joaquin spoke. It sounded like he was getting out of bed.

"Joaquin, stop worrying. I have work in the morning."

"Then, I'll drive you, sweetheart," Joaquin insisted, and I smiled.

"You'll probably drive me and stay with me all day."

"I don't see a problem with that," Joaquin stated.

"The problem is that you can't fix everything."

"I won't bother you; I'll even sleep on the couch," he joked, and I knew that would never happen.

"No, you'll stay home, and I will talk to you later. Goodbye," I said then hung up the call.

...

The next day I was looking at my calendar and emails with Cassidy before I headed home. Cassidy typed on her computer as I read over my schedule and poured myself some water.

"Sofia! Sofia!" Cassidy yelled out, and I realized I was making a mess as water spilled over the glass.

"Sorry."

"Are you okay?" Cassidy questioned.

"Huh."

"You seem distracted," Cassidy mentioned, and I stood up, walked to the bathroom and grabbed a paper towel to clean up my mess.

"I had a nightmare last night."

"You want to talk about it?" Cassidy asked, and I shook my head no.

"No, Joaquin wanted to come over and talk, but I'll be fine."

"If you change your mind, let me know."

"Thanks, but work is all I need," I replied and tossed the towels in the trash and continued to read over what I needed to get a handle on before my career got overshadowed by my personal life.

...

Two days later.

I woke up refreshed today knowing I would be leaving the hospital. Joaquin came in last night to spend the night on the couch after my parents left. Neither of them spoke to him and the tension could've been cut with a knife. Doctor Johnson came back yesterday afternoon and explained that all the tests came back fine, and I was clear to head home, but I still needed to rest and take things slow. I was too far along with filming and recording my album to stop the momentum. I asked Chauncey if he could come to my apartment to run through some songs together and Cassidy would be coming over to figure out a plan for my schedule. Social media was nonstop about my shooting and the reason I was in the hospital; some people said I was pregnant or having cosmetic surgery. I wanted to curse Joaquin out for bringing all this drama into my life. Nurse Naomi helped me out of the wheelchair and Joaquin assisted me into the car. I looked up front and saw Hugo was driving. My eyes peered at Joaquin and he assured me Hugo could be trusted, but we thought the same thing about Leonardo and look at how that turned out. The car door closed after Joaquin slid inside and helped me with my seatbelt. He grasped my hand as the car turned into traffic.

"Did they find Leonardo?"

"He's nothing to worry about," Joaquin said, then lifted my hand to press a kiss to my palm.

While he was with me last night, we mainly watched tv and avoided talking about the events that occurred on the boat. I knew it was coming, though, and my stomach clenched in dread.

"He never touched me," I blurted out and waited for his response.

"I know."

"I prayed that you would save me, and things would go back to normal."

"Things would never be normal, Sofia, once I stepped into your life."

"I see that now."

"Do you have regrets?" Joaquin asked as he cupped my chin to stare into my eyes.

I shook my head no.

"I love you, but we need to talk about where things go from here," I responded, sitting back against the seat as he picked my legs up to massage my feet.

"We move forward together, starting with you moving in with me," Joaquin spoke and my eyes widened in shock.

"What are you talking about?"

"I want you to move in with me."

"Do I have a choice?"

"Sweetheart, you always have a choice, but it's for your protection and my peace of mind."

"You prefer we live together," I stated.

"Yes. Gael found a few places we can go check out this weekend," Joaquin replied as the car stopped in front of my apartment building. I saw Cassidy and Chauncey standing outside.

"What are they doing here?" Joaquin asked as he helped me out of the car.

"I wanted to record some songs. I still need to work, Joaquin," I fussed, pushing him out of the way to walk ahead of him.

"Sweetheart...Sofia, stop walking," he demanded and I stopped.

"Are we interrupting?" Cassidy asked.

"Yes," Joaquin said.

"No, come on up and we can get started." I ignored him and walked them through the lobby and to the elevator.

"How are you feeling, Sofia? I heard about what happened," Chauncey asked.

"Still tired but recovering slowly."

"Glad to hear it, and what about your boyfriend? Is he cool with us being here?" Chauncey inquired.

"This is my home," I said as the elevator doors opened and we stepped off. I walked to my door and unlocked it, sighing in relief at the instantaneous comfort I felt just stepping inside. Feelings of being back home in my own space did something to me. I took a seat on the couch, picked up the pillow and held it against my chest.

"Should we order food? I know you're not up to cooking," Cassidy questioned.

"That's fine, but tell me about Edward. Any news on him?" Cassidy started to answer when Joaquin stalked inside and glared at me.

"Come talk to me," Joaquin said.

"I'm busy," I responded.

"Sofia, if you expect to have a peaceful evening you need to come and speak with me right now," Joaquin said. I rolled my eyes and jumped up and marched to the back of the apartment away from Cassidy and Chauncey.

"What do you want?"

Joaquin pulled me into his chest, and I hugged him back automatically. He brushed his lips against my shoulder blade, up my neck and down my cheek toward my lips.

"Stop fighting me, sweetheart, I only want the best for you."

"Do you love me?" I questioned.

"Yes. What kind of question is that?"

"Then tell me about Edward."

He sighed and removed his hands from around my waist and sat on the edge of the bed.

"I plan on killing him if I see him," he said and shrugged his shoulders like it was the simplest thing in the world.

"Baby you can't kill him."

"Are you defending him?" Joaquin shouted.

"No, are you crazy? Listen, I want more than anything to see the bastard dead, but he's a very important person. Let the police handle him."

"Sofia, putting the police on him would be a piece of cake. I want him dead now."

"Joaquin."

"No more talking, you need to rest, and I have to leave and handle some business," Joaquin said.

"Are you coming back tonight?" I inquired while I tugged at my earlobe nervously knowing that Edward would be dead soon and it was all my fault.

"I am so don't be long. I want you in bed resting."

"I promise."

"Perfect, I'll leave Alex and Hugo here with you." Joaquin's eyes implored me not to fight him on getting revenge.

"Okay."

He stood and kissed me again and left the bedroom. I followed behind and saw Hugo and Alex already at the door.

"Cassidy, can you order enough food for Alex and Hugo as well please?" I asked and she nodded in answer.

"Joaquin, don't forget what we talked about." He smiled as he strolled out of the apartment as Alex and Hugo stood at the door watching us.

"You guys don't need to stand. Take a seat or something."

"Boss wants us by your side at all times," Hugo mentioned.

"Hugo, please it makes me nervous."

"We'll be outside, call us if you need anything," Hugo stated.

"Thanks."

"Okay, so that was the director. He put a hold on the movie until you're fully recovered," Cassidy commented, and I kicked off my shoes and laid back on the couch.

"First thing I need Cassidy to do is to get my schedule updated. I want to get back to work."

"What about Edward?"

"Fuck Edward, that motherfucker was in on trying to kidnap me."

Cassidy and Chauncey both gasped in surprise.

"Sofia, you can't be serious," Cassidy said.

"Serious as a heart attack."

"I can't believe he would do something so vile," Cassidy stated, wiping away a tear before it fell down her cheek.

"You're not the only one, but Joaquin told me the guy that kidnapped me had help."

"So, Edward wanted you dead. For what reason though?" Cassidy questioned.

"That's some crazy shit, man," Chauncey responded.

"Chauncey, you haven't been around my personal life the way Cassidy is, but Edward wanted me and I rejected him."

"So he decides to plan a kidnapping." Chauncey wrung his hands in front of his body.

"I don't know what he thought he was doing, but he's fired now."

Hugo peeked through the door holding a bag of food. Cassidy took it from him and put everything on the table and I stood up to get plates and utensils from the kitchen. I picked up some bottles of water since I was still recovering and needed to be alert without alcohol in my system. I passed Cassidy and Chauncey the water, she gave me a plate of ribs, baked beans, mac and cheese, and greens. I had my cheat days and it started today until filming started back up.

"I never knew how much I needed this until now," I muttered as I stuffed my face with more baked beans.

"I know you may not think I'm good enough, but what about me managing you?" Cassidy asked.

"That's a lot of responsibility, Cassidy."

"I mean I already help with so much now. I think I can handle more," Cassidy said.

"She helps with the concerts, way more than Edward ever did," Chauncey responded.

"Am I still set for Expressive Designs? I know I missed the launch because of the mess with Joaquin."

"Yeah, I just told the owner you had a family emergency pop up a few days before the launch," Cassidy said.

"Great, put in a call and set a meeting for later this week."

"What about your album?" Chauncey asked.

"Push it back, everything that Edward is behind I want removed," I demanded then took a bite of the short rib.

"What do you think of a photoshoot and interview letting the world know you're back?" Cassidy asked.

"That's fine, do the shoot with a magazine that's friendly to us."

"I have some songs I wrote that I haven't given to anyone else," Chauncey stated, gulping the rest of his water.

"Let me hear them."

"The demo starts a little slow, but it picks up." Chauncey hit the button on his computer and a smooth melody came through. It sounded more jazz and blues rather than old school R&B. I bobbed my head to the lyrics of a woman singing about not needing love anymore and coming into her own.

"I like that, I would want the second verse a little harder."

"That's fine," Chauncey stated.

I grabbed my phone, and checked social media as we continued talking about new changes.

CHAPTER 6

Sofia

"Hey, Ma," I answered, pointing to a cute dress Cassidy was showing me on her iPad.

"We're back at the hotel, baby. Your father and I wanted to check in on you."

"I'm fine, just sitting here with Cassidy and Chauncey."

"Is that boyfriend of yours around?" she questioned, and I blew out a breath of frustration.

"No, but I want you to have lunch with us this week-end," I stated.

"I'll talk to your father and see how he feels about it," Mom said.

"Thanks, but we know how stubborn your husband can get," I joked before I reached over and grabbed another piece of rib out of the box.

"Keep me updated, sweetie and we'll check in later," Mom said.

"When is your flight back?"

"This weekend, so try not to get caught up with work so we can spend some time together," Mom suggested.

"Okay. Let me call you when I figure out my plans," I said and hung up the phone.

I chuckled thinking about my father fussing about his little girl. That man had been my protector forever and now that someone new was in the picture he'd had to step back. I finished eating and checked the time on my phone then strolled to the kitchen to clean up. I started singing the lyrics to the song that Chauncey played when we heard yelling and gunshots.

Pop! Pop!

"OMG!" Cassidy screamed and dropped to the floor. Chauncey followed suit and I ran back to my couch and grabbed my phone to call Joaquin. As soon as I started to dial his number the door burst open and the man that I now knew as Ciro was standing there.

"We meet again, Miss Chambers," Ciro stated.

"Let them go, it's me you want," I pleaded, speed dialing Joaquin's number. I had him saved as my number one emergency contact.

"Kind of sad your boyfriend left you alone again," Ciro said.

"What's sad is a man taking out his revenge on a woman that had nothing to do with your niece," I spat.

He grinned as he marched into my house with two more men behind him.

"Where's Edward?" I questioned.

"Your little manager friend is hiding from me," Ciro said.

"Look, Joaquin is not here."

"We have some unfinished business, Sofia," Ciro said as he ran his hand across my cheek.

"What happened to Hugo and Alex?"

"They're fine, unless you come with me now."

"No," I said before I head butted him and ran to the

kitchen where I grabbed a knife. He was a little dazed, but I was able to put some distance between us. One of his men grabbed Cassidy by the arm and stood her up.

"If you don't want anything to happen to your little friend," Ciro threatened through gritted teeth.

"Let them go first," I responded as I waved the knife back and forth.

"I'm running this show, Miss Chambers," Ciro said.

I glanced over at Chauncey and one of the guys kicked him in the stomach.

"Stop!" I yelled.

"That's for disobeying me," Ciro said.

"You son of a bitch." I lunged at him and he caught my wrist and twisted my hand making me drop the knife. I clenched my left hand and punched him in the nose and kneed him in the balls.

"You bitch!" Ciro shouted and tried to grab for me again and I picked up his gun.

"I'm only going to say this once. Let my friends go or I'll kill you."

"Sofia! Sofia!" I heard Joaquin call out.

"In here!" I replied. He rushed through the door with Gabriella and Gael. It was a full-on standoff in the room. Cassidy and Chauncey were bystanders in the bullshit of my life that came with dating Joaquin.

"Baby put the gun down," Joaquin said and I shook my head no.

"I want him to leave and take his men with him," I said as tears fell down my cheeks.

"You have no idea who you're messing with, little girl," Ciro stated. I shot a little above his head and everyone ducked.

"Get out," I snapped then pointed the gun right in between his eyes. I grew up in the South; I wasn't afraid of guns. My father taught me how to protect myself, I just chose not to carry a gun in New York.

"I can handle it from here, sweetheart," Joaquin stated, before he motioned for them all to leave. They released Chauncey and Cassidy while Gael checked on Hugo outside of the door. Joaquin started to come toward me and I held my hand up to stop him.

"Leave."

"What?"

"I said leave, Joaquin. This is too much for me."

"You don't get to decide that," Joaquin spat.

"Like hell I don't, they just burst into my home and tried to kill me and my friends."

"Sofia, baby, you're scared, I get that. Leaving me is not an option," Joaquin said. He tried to come close and I held the gun up. His eyes widened in surprise.

"Sofia," Gael said.

"No, I want you gone. My life was simple before this bullshit came around."

"I'm not leaving you."

"Then I'll leave." I started to walk off and he grabbed my arm stopping me.

"Wait! Wait... Shushhhh."

"Just go, Joaquin."

"I'll give you some space, but we're not through."

"Take care of Hugo," I stated and placed Ciro's gun in his hand. I ran over to Chauncey and Cassidy to make sure they were okay. Gael talked Joaquin into leaving before he blew up even further. I could see in his eyes when everything went blank that he was ready to become this Ghost person. Maybe my parents were right, and I needed to get the police involved, because Ciro didn't care where I lived and who I was with. All he wanted was to get revenge by any means for his dead niece. Everyone left and an hour later I was soaking in the tub with my eyes closed thinking about how I went from preparing to go out to dinner with my boyfriend on a boat to being kidnapped, shot at, jumped in freezing cold temperatures. Rescued then almost kidnapped again. I could probably write a book about my life at this point. I pulled the plug and stepped out, dried off and removed the wrap from around my hair. I already brushed my teeth before getting in the tub, so I just lotioned up and jumped into bed then checked a few messages.

Joaquin: I'll give you space for now.

Me: It doesn't work like that.

Joaquin: Try me.

I let out a harsh breath and turned my light off in my bedroom and sunk deeper under the covers. I wouldn't let Joaquin's possessive ways get to me any longer. My mind was made up and I might even start to see other people.

Joaquin: Goodnight beautiful.

...

The next morning I blinked my eyes open slowly, feeling like someone was watching me. I adjusted in the bed, wiped the crust out of my eyes, and looked over to the couch under the window. I got it several months ago so I'd have something for me to sit on and read. I jumped when I saw Joaquin staring back at me, wearing the same clothes from yesterday.

"What are you doing here?" I muttered groggily, sitting up against the headboard.

"I needed to make sure you were safe."

"No, you're doing the control bullshit again. I'm fine, you can leave now."

He leaned over, clasping his hands together.

"You know why I pursued you?" Joaquin asked as he stared into my eyes.

I turned my head, not wanting to deal with more stress. I was planning on meeting with Cassidy today at a photo studio to get my life started back up and running.

"Joaquin."

"I wanted you the moment I saw your smile," he spoke.

"What do you mean? We only bumped into each other at the restaurant."

"I stood outside of the door and watched you have lunch with Edward for a few minutes and something made you smile. Your presence stilled me, calmed the noise in my head," Joaquin stated and stood up slowly.

"I think it's best we both focus on other things and get space. I need to get my career on track," I said, pushed the covers back, stood up and made the bed.

"You can have your space, but I want you to have security at all times."

"That's not necessary," I replied as I walked to the bathroom and turned the light on.

"Edward is still involved somehow and Ciro is still missing," Joaquin responded, standing at the door of the bathroom.

I started to brush my hair up into a bun then tied a scarf around it to keep it from getting wet.

We stared at each other through the mirror.

"I trust you'll find him, but I'm not stopping my life or career."

"Sofia," he groaned and started to come closer. I held my hand up to stop him from getting closer to talk me out of wanting space.

"Cassidy is meeting me at the studio, I can't do this with you right now," I told him, and removed my nightshirt, standing naked in front of him as I closed the door in his face.

An hour later I jumped out of the cab and headed inside of the photo studio texting Cassidy to make sure she was here.

"Sofia!" Cassidy called out.

I waved and she came over with the designer of the clothing brand we signed a contract with to become their brand ambassador. With me going back into the studios, and finally getting back into acting, hopefully I could put this nightmare of the past few days behind me.

"Hey Maggie, thanks again for pushing back the shoot," I said, removing my jacket. She was around my age, maybe a few years older. Shorter in height and with an athletic build, she reminded me of a younger Serena Williams mixed with Jill Scott. Someone that loved working out, but was still laid-back and doesn't get overly stressed about things.

"When we heard everything that was happening, we wanted to make sure your safety and recovery was first," Maggie, the owner and designer of Expressive Designs, said.

"Maggie and the team were really supportive and sent flowers to the hospital," Cassidy remarked. I held my hand up to my heart thanking her for the support.

"What's the plan for today? Cassidy said you looked at the notes we sent over."

"Yes we did and I know you recently came out of the hospital so we'll need to do alterations in the moment," she replied and we headed to through the lobby of the photography studio that Expressive Designs built for their company. The colors matched the brand with maroon, orange, and black. The front held a wall display with mannequins wearing the latest fashions. There was a huge tv on the wall with the fashion show that debuted the collection. She escorted us back to the makeup area. It brought back memories of the situation with the bomb scare and I felt a little jittery, but I didn't want to alarm anyone and end the shoot before it started.

"Today is mostly shots of you wearing each outfit as a test look," Maggie said, showing off the pieces that were hanging on the rack next to us. The photographer was setting up shots with his crew as the makeup artist strolled in from the back employee section with more lights.

"Bridget, you remember Sofia and Cassidy right?" Maggie asked and Bridget held her hand out and we shook.

"I'm a huge fan of yours, Sofia. Are you working on another album?" Bridget asked.

"Most definitely am, my fans have hounded me enough," I joked as we all laughed in conjunction.

Cassidy stood on the right side of me with her phone and iPad out.

"I forwarded all of your emails to me now. So far, I've spoken with your lawyer and accountants," Cassidy rattled off.

"Can I get some water?" I asked Cassidy and she grabbed a bottle of water from the craft table.

For today's shoot the setup was a white and gold backdrop with me standing in the front of the Expressive Designs logo.

"I have the first two outfits. A legging one-piece jumper set that we can interchange," Maggie commented, holding up the two outfits.

"I didn't need to do too much on you, Sofia. You can get dressed now," Bridget said.

"Perfect, thanks, Bridget." I took another sip of water and stood up, grabbed the pantsuit and walked into the dressing room to change.

I slipped on the maroon and black suit with the side belts hanging and large pockets. The wardrobe stylist dropped down to the floor to help me slip on the shoes, then touched up my hair.

"We're ready for you, Sofia," Tobias, the photographer, said and I strolled toward the front of the backdrop. Cassidy took shots on her phone for social media.

Tobias motioned for me to put my hands on my waist and turn to the left side, while looking directly into the camera. The flash of the camera went off as the music turned on with Jazzmen Sullivan playing in the background.

"Nice, Sofia, like that, keep going," Tobias said as he turned the camera sideways then moved in closer toward me.

I squatted down on my knees with my hands on top, looking directly into the camera.

"Stay like that, show you're a badass," Tobias announced.

"Let me get a photo we can use for your social media header," Cassidy insisted. She walked next to the photographer to grab the shot.

"Check out what we have so far," Maggie remarked, standing behind the video monitor.

Bridget strolled over and checked my makeup and passed me a bottle of water. I felt renewed and vibrant with getting things moving in the right direction for my career.

"Cassidy, can you pass my phone please?" I said.

"Sure, here you go," Cassidy replied. She marched to my purse, lifted my phone out of my purse and brought it to me. I checked for messages and nothing was there from Joaquin so I guessed he got the message that I wanted to be alone and focus on my work.

"Anything major?" Cassidy wondered, taking the phone back.

"Nope, quiet thank goodness. Maggie should I change?" I questioned.

"Yep, do the sports bra and pants," Maggie responded as she grabbed the pants and shirt for me to change.

I slipped into the dressing room and changed into the next outfit while Tobias set up the next shot. It had more lighting and a short box for me to step up on.

"Sofia, can I get you to put one foot up on the box and turn your body facing the wall?" Tobias asked.

Once I was in the position he requested, I checked to make sure my breasts looked good then smoothed my hand down to make sure all the lint was gone.

"Ready," I said.

Tobias picked up the camera again and started taking shots. I put my right arm on top of my left, then smiled into the camera.

"Looking good, Sofia," Tobias said. Bridget stepped into the frame to add gold bronzer to my back. The next four hours went well and everyone decided to go out and have a few drinks together to celebrate. It was me, Maggie, Cassidy, Tobias, and Bridget that jumped into his car and headed to Bar One. I put the hood over my head to keep the photographers from noticing me as the crowd grew bigger.

"Welcome to Bar One. Are you looking for a booth or did you want to sit at the bar?" the hostess stated.

Bar One was the spot that all of Hollywood and the music industry came to hang out. They had it decorated with clear glass throughout the room. Gold lights hung throughout the club. The bar sat in the middle of the entire room with four televisions mounted around and the DJ had his own stage set up in the corner pumping music.

"Booth please," Maggie said, and the hostess motioned for us to follow her to the back booth in the corner.

"OMG! It's Sofia Chambers." A girl wearing next to nothing in a skimpy dress tried to come over for a hug and Tobias blocked her from moving in close.

CHAPTER 7

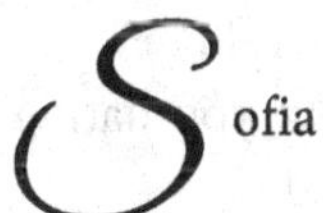

Sofia

I SCOOTED into the corner and Tobias squeezed in next to me. The hostess placed drink menus down for us as the bass of the music started to pick up. Different strobe lights flashed around the room with women getting up out of their seats. I could see people in the VIP area in the top level throwing drinks in the air.

"Today was great, Sofia, we need to set up another one with you," Tobias muttered in my ear over the loud music.

"Set it up with Cassidy, I like the way you guys work and don't hang around wasting time," I said, as the hostess brought over a bottle of Ace of Spades and a martini.

"We didn't order this," Cassidy said to the hostess.

"This was a gift from the owner," the hostess said.

"Who's the owner?" Tobias queried, happily opening the bottle.

"Mr. Fuertes," she said, and I almost spit the drink out.

Everybody peered at me while I scanned the room trying to see if Joaquin was nearby.

"Is he here?" I asked her.

"No, he saw you on the monitor remotely," she replied.

"That's your boyfriend, right?" Tobias questioned.

"No. It's a complicated situation," I replied.

"We saw on the news about your kidnapping," Bridget brought up and Maggie glared at her.

"What?" Bridget asked. Her expression was perplexed as if she couldn't understand why Maggie would be upset.

She didn't seem like the type of person that was aloof or just gossiped about things back at the studio; now that we were not on set she must have felt more comfortable.

"That's not your business, Bridget," Maggie told her.

"Sorry, I mean it's all over the news about you dating some big time cartel boss," Bridget commented.

"The media is always twisting stories," I said.

"We should make a toast, to a successful launch and new album, Sofia," Cassidy said, raising her glass in the air. The rest of us joined in and clinked glasses. I chuckled at Cassidy dancing in her seat.

"Come on, Sofia, you should let loose a little," Cassidy suggested and pointed to the dance floor.

"I'm not really dressed to be seen. You go ahead... I'll stay relaxing with a drink." I sipped the rest of the dry martini down and waved for the bar girl to bring me another one.

"I'll go with you," Bridget responded and Maggie let Cassidy out of the booth and the three of them switched to the dance floor.

"You have to excuse Bridget," Tobias commented.

"She's curious like everyone else. No worries," I responded. Maggie and I continued glancing around, observing the other patrons.

Tobias stretched his arm out on the back of the booth and smiled. He was tall with a nicely trimmed beard, full lips, and dark brown skin. He reminded me of the actor Morris Chestnut with the low cut waves.

"Tell me about yourself, Sofia," Tobias said.

"Not much to tell, I'm an actress and singer. Trying to make it in New York," I responded.

"What do you find harder, singing, or acting?" Tobias investigated, nudging me in the arm.

"Probably singing, since it's more intimate."

"You do have a beautiful voice," Tobias replied and smiled.

"Are you flirting with me?"

"Is it working?" he replied as we both broke out in laughter.

My eyes raised in shock when Hugo and Gael stepped in front of the booth. I looked around for Joaquin wondering if he saw us and thought this was a date. Gael cleared his throat and glared at Tobias.

"How are you, Sofia?" Gael asked.

"Gael, no."

"He's not here. We just wanted to make sure you're okay, with your new friend," Gael spoke.

"Who are you?" Tobias asked while trying to stand up out of the booth. Hugo pushed him back down.

"Hey!" Tobias shouted.

"I wouldn't raise my voice in someone's business establishment, sir," Gael suggested with a harsh glare on his face.

"Gael, I'm hanging with friends. Tell him to back off."

"You know we can't do that," Gael answered.

"Ohh, look what we have here," Monica said as she walked up with a group of women behind her.

"I don't have time for this." I rubbed the temples of my forehead.

"Monica, you know you're not allowed here," Gael said.

"I can do what I want, Gael, Joaquin doesn't run me like his little bitch over there," Monica spat, and I tried to jump up and punch her in the face. Tobias held me around the waist and pulled me back down.

"Is this the new boyfriend? I guess you couldn't take Joaquin's lifestyle," Monica responded.

"Get out of here," Gael said.

"No, I'll leave. I had no idea he owned this place," I said.

"Sofia, we can go somewhere else," Tobias mentioned, getting out of the booth to help me up. I didn't have the heart to tell him that I was very much still in love with Joaquin. Dating anyone new right now wouldn't help me at all with the press still hounding me and me trying to get back to work.

"She's not leaving with you," Gael announced and stepped in front of Tobias.

"Tobias, he's right. I can't leave with you. I'll be fine."

"Are you sure?" Tobias queried; Hugo tried to shove him away when he grasped my elbow.

"Hugo, stop it!" I shouted and pointed at Gael.

"Tobias we'll talk. Send Cassidy the edits for approval."

"Hey, are you leaving?" Cassidy came over, fanning herself.

"Yeah, I'm tired, and it's getting crowded," I fussed as I rolled my eyes at Monica who was whispering in her friend's ear and laughing.

"I'll leave with you," Cassidy said, and grabbed her things off the table.

"I have a car out front," Gael stated as he motioned to follow him and I stormed out to the car he had out front. He chuckled and I wanted to smack that smirk off his face.

"Have you talked to Alessandra?" I asked and the smirk washed off his face.

"You play, Sofia," Gael spoke as he opened the door for me to get inside. I looked around to make sure Joaquin wasn't there.

"I haven't talked to her since before the kidnapping."

He closed the door and walked around to the passenger of the SUV and Hugo slid the key into the ignition and drove off into traffic.

"She moved here to the city. She's taking fashion classes," Gael said.

"Oh."

"What's your name?" Cassidy remarked as she tapped Hugo on the shoulder.

"He doesn't like to talk," Gael responded, and Hugo looked through the rearview mirror at Cassidy. I wanted to laugh at the grimace that had crossed Hugo's face at Gael's answer. Cassidy seemed to not care at all because she checked her makeup in the mirror.

"Finally."

"Let Hugo walk you up," Gael said, and I shook my head no.

"We'll be fine and make sure to tell your friend he doesn't have to send drinks over anymore," I said. Cassidy opened the rear passenger side door and I climbed out.

"Sofia, you're being unreasonable," Gael said as he leaned over the car door.

"I might be, but your boy should keep his little fling under control."

"You know she doesn't mean anything to him," Gael told me.

"Goodnight, Gael." I waved him off and stalked in the apartment building with Cassidy behind me.

Cassidy came in behind me and dropped down on the

couch and I locked the door, kicked my shoes off and dropped my jacket on the couch. I headed to the kitchen and grabbed a bottle of water to work through the alcohol.

"You can crash in the guest bedroom," I said and shut the fridge.

"Uhhh...huh," Cassidy replied, snorting a little as I laughed. I strolled to my bedroom with my purse to check for any messages. I took my phone out and saw Joaquin had sent a text message.

Joaquin: Dinner tomorrow.

Me: No.

Joaquin: You have fun tonight?

Me: Goodnight Joaquin.

CHAPTER 8

*J*oaquin
A month later.

THE LAST TIME I spoke to her was the night I texted to go
out to dinner. I wanted to work on what was broken
between us and figure out a compromise. In her mind we
were broken up, but I let her think this for now until she
was fully healed from everything. After today there would
be no more being apart now that I'd found a home for us to
live together. There was so much going on in my life from
my sister living here now to my parents constantly
wanting to know what my plans were with Sofia. Surprisingly my father was coming around to liking Sofia now
and I'd been told my sister had hung out with Sofia and
Cassidy a few times since she moved back here. Today I
woke up with an agenda and a plan to end the drama in
Sofia's and my life for good. It would only happen after I
took out the trash that kept popping up so I called to have
dinner with Monica and she jumped at the chance to see

me again. When I got word she was at Bar One and got in Sofia's face I wanted to strangle her right then and there if I didn't already have a plan to get rid of any obstacles that stood in our way as a couple. I had Gael and Hugo already at the bar doing a drop off, and I had cameras set up on my phone to monitor all my businesses. To see Sofia walk in with another man was a hit to my ego, but I needed to stay calm and not overreact like I usually did. The plan for today should be enough to show Sofia I was serious about what I wanted and nothing would get in the middle of us ever again. The car stopped in front of Antonio's with Hugo and Gael following me inside.

"Make sure you call your sister. Something about dinner as a family," Gael spoke, as the door opened and I buttoned my suit jacket. I had Bruno close the restaurant down for me to have this conversation privately. I noticed Monica in the back at the private section with a closed off door, but the window was glass. People could only see in the back, but not hear.

"Is she all right?"

"She's having lunch with Sofia," Gael said and I nodded in excitement. Alessandra knew how much Sofia meant to me and if she could convince her to put the past behind us, then I wouldn't have to have more bloodshed in the city.

"Text and tell her to check my calendar," I responded as I slid the door of the private room to the side and Monica grinned before she stood up to give me a kiss as I motioned to stay seated.

"I missed you, Joaquin," Monica whined as she licked her lips.

"Give us a few minutes, Gael, before we order lunch."

Gael turned and left the room to stand at the door.

"I knew you would be back," Monica stated, shifting her glass of wine back and forth.

"You're right."

Monica extended her hand and stroked the top of my palm.

"So that means you're finished with that tramp Sofia," Monica said.

"Do you enjoy the wine?" I questioned as I pushed the glass closer toward her.

"I did, it's one of my favorites. You remembered, baby," Monica spoke while a nervous smile played along the edges of her full lips.

"Always remember a predictable bitch."

"Whattt..." Monica stuttered in shock.

"In about a minute your body should lock up on you. Because of the drug I had put in your wine."

Her eyes popped wide.

"What did you do?" She tried to lift her hand to her throat but was frozen in place.

"It's an odorless, tasteless drug that should keep you from moving so my men can take you away without restraint."

A tear started to fall down her check.

"Please..." Monica whispered slowly, her lips not moving.

"All you had to do was leave things alone. What we had was only sex."

A small screech started to come through her voice.

"Save your voice. They can't hear you and even if they did, no one is coming."

The door opened with Hugo and Gael coming inside and I lifted her up out of the seat by her arms as her eyes darted back and forth in fear.

"How much did you give her?" Gael questioned.

"Enough to stabilize her until you get her to the warehouse."

"I paid off a photographer and got word that Edward was out in New Jersey," Gael spoke, carrying Monica out the back of the restaurant.

Carlo came from the back of the office with some papers in his hand.

"What's all this?" Carlo inquired as Hugo loaded Monica in the back of the white van.

"Taking out the trash."

"You get word on Ciro and her ex manager?" Carlo asked.

"Headed to the third stop now," I said and started to walk out through the exit.

"Try to keep your emotions under control, Joaquin!" Carlo yelled out and I waved him off.

I jumped in the second car with Gael as we followed Hugo and Gabriella in the white van.

"She misses you," Gael announced through the silence.

"Did you send a message to her little photographer friend?" I asked.

They turned down the street heading onto the freeway.

"A quiet message, but deadly warning," Gael responded, and I pulled my phone out of my pocket to see a message from Sofia.

My wife: You're a complete asshole.

I smirked at her text message.

Me: How can that be if we haven't spoken in a month?

My wife: Gael threatened Tobias.

Me: I had nothing to do with that.

My wife: I don't believe you.

Me: Go out to dinner with me.

My wife: I have dinner plans already.

Seeing her reply about having dinner plans caused a lump in my throat. Maybe it was with my sister and I was overreacting.

Me: With who?

My wife: None of your business asshole.

Me: Sofia, I don't like secrets, beautiful.

My wife: Good, because I don't like arrogant, jealous, assholes that try to boss me around.

"Ughhh..." I groaned and closed out of my text messages to check her location from the tracker. It showed she was on set filming. She might have made that statement to throw me off and get under my skin.

Me: Soon we'll be together again.

My wife: No. I'm done with you and you can tell all of your henchmen to stay away.

I chuckled at her last text and closed out of my phone as the car stopped at a house out in the suburbs of New Jersey. It was mid-day so the neighbors weren't going to be around to hear anything or see anything they shouldn't.

"He should be coming out to take the trash to the curb. You want us to grab him then?" Gael asked.

"Is that his car in the driveway?" I questioned, seeing a black Lexus jeep parked.

"Yeah, based on the license plate he got it two months ago," Gael responded.

"Have Hugo slash the tires and cut all the lights out," I said, opening the glove compartment to grab my black gloves and silencer.

"We're taking him alive right?" Gael asked.

"Depends on how I feel when I see his face." I shrugged, opened the car door, stepped out and looked around.

I walked around to the back of the house with Gael while Hugo went to slash the tires and Gabriella stood at the front door monitoring things. I peered through the side window, noticed it was the kitchen and his back was to me. I motioned for Gael to follow and we headed to the back door and slowly slid it open since the music was loud and he was obviously in his own thoughts. I eased into the hallway, looked to my right, then left to see if another person was around. Feeling more confident that the place was secure, I tapped Gael to check the rest of the house while I confronted Edward. I strolled into the kitchen calmly and he still wasn't noticing anything while the music was blasting loud. I turned the button down low and he jumped in fright.

"Shit!" Edward shouted.

"Edward."

"Uh… I can explain," Edward said.

"Can you?" I questioned and sat down at the kitchen table.

"Listen, I was looking out for Sofia's safety. Ciro said he worked for you," Edward told me.

I grinned, letting him fall into more rabbit holes of lies. Gael made an appearance on the other side of Edward as he tried to back up out of the kitchen.

"Edward have a seat."

"I…I…please, man," Edward stated, fidgeting with his hands.

"Edward, I wasn't asking."

Gael pushed him forward and Edward took a seat in front of me.

"I think we got off on the wrong foot. Do you agree?"

Edward looked behind himself, then back at me.

"Yes."

"The one thing I asked you to do was not to get involved in my business."

"I didn't know he would kidnap Sofia," Edward explained.

"Silence!" I slammed my hand on the top of the table.

"Please don't kill me, I'm a high-profile person. The cops will come looking for you," Edward said before he tried to rush to grab the butter knife. I grabbed his wrist and twisted it back.

"Aghhh!!! Please..." Edward screamed, falling to the floor.

"Gael," I said and he stalked over and stabbed Edward with the same poison in his neck.

"We need to hurry up before Monica comes out of it," Gael mentioned and I agreed.

"The faster we get this done, the sooner we can get Ciro finished."

Gael and I lifted Edward off the floor, carried his body through the front door and put him inside the van. The house was locked up by Gabriella as we loaded up to leave.

...

Two hours later I was sitting with both Monica and Edward hung up on chains naked in my warehouse. I stared at them both as they started to come out of the poison. They still couldn't move, but they could talk.

"Arghhh...Joaquin, I love you," Monica screamed and cried trying to get me to let her go. I picked up the machete and walked up to Monica as she tried to get out of the chains, but there was no leaving this building besides in a body bag.

"You had your chance, now you must die."

"Please...I beg you, let me go and you won't hear from me again," Monica pleaded as I ran my hand across her thigh. I used to enjoy what was between them, but the sight only brought misery and regret now.

"That I doubt, but I will give you a choice."

"Anything, I'll take it," Monica said, not knowing what I was about to bring up.

"Then you'll die second." I waved the machete in the air.

"Ahhh…" she gasped as I plunged the machete across Edward's chest. As blood spilled out, Monica started crying and throwing up as Edward screamed and passed out.

"No one can hear you, Monica." I took Edward's legs off, then dropped the machete to the floor, wiped the sweat off with the handkerchief from my pocket.

"Joaquin, you know me," Monica cried out as I started to walk toward her.

"You know I don't tolerate disrespect." I grasped the bottom of her chin and stared into her eyes.

"I don't want to die," Monica whimpered.

"Should have thought about that before confronting my wife."

"You…You…Aghhhh," she screamed as the snake I picked up out of the box that Gael brought out and placed next to her feet slid around.

"Don't fight it, let it happen naturally," I said as I placed the snake in a bag. Gael lowered her down from the chain and the bag went over her head as she screamed and cried.

"Aghhhh…" Monica twitched, then her limp body fell over.

"Finish her off," I said and left the warehouse to hop in my car to go home and shower. Forty minutes after making it home at the new house I received a message from my tech guy that Ciro was spotted coming out of the hotel. Antonio said his people were watching him and this was my chance to grab him without interruption.

I dialed Gael's number while I hopped in the shower.

"Yeah," Gael said, with loud music coming through the phone.

"Our guest arrived today," I said in code through the phone.

"Perfect, I'll have dinner reservations texted to you,"

Gael responded and hung up before I could ask about the music in the background. I had a weird feeling so I called my sister.

"Joaquin! I miss you," Alessandra said excitedly. Loud background music made it difficult to hear her.

"Where are you, Alessandra?" I questioned, giving her a chance to be honest.

"Out with friends," she replied.

"What friends?" I turned the knob up hotter, to let the steam fill the room.

"Some friends from school," Alessandra spoke.

"We'll do lunch and I want to meet these friends," I said.

"Joaquin."

"Yes, princess?"

"I have to tell you something," Alessandra muttered lowly.

"Over lunch, we'll talk and tell your friend or friends that if you're hurt in any way…"

"I'm fine and my friend is sweet."

"I'll talk to you later," I said and hung up.

CHAPTER 9

*J*oaquin

MIDNIGHT.

I WAS PARKED outside of Sofia's apartment fresh from getting changed and showered. My thoughts were on hearing my sister over the phone wanting to meet for lunch and tell me something that I already suspected. The thought of her being with a man that was like me, and I thought of as a brother had caused a knot in my stomach. Gael was just as ruthless and only leveled me out when I went too far, but we had many years of drinking, women, and killings between us. Now to see him possibly want to start something with my little sister was unnerving.

I removed the key out of the car, got out and headed into her building. I nodded at the receptionist and security guard. I'd paid them to keep an eye on when she comes and goes. The people that enter the building had all been checked out with a background report. After the shit with Edward I wasn't taking another chance on something else happening to her until I could convince her to move with me to our new house. I stepped on the elevator, hit the button for her floor as the doors closed and I saw my reflection in the door. I was a man that was relentless and heartless for the past few years until she stepped into my life.

Beep!

The elevator dinged and I got off chuckling at her probably being in bed snoring. I pulled the key I had made out, opened the door, then locked it behind me.

I removed my jacket and kicked my shoes off in the hallway.

Her door was partially open, but her light was off. I slowly eased inside and watched as her chest moved up and down slowly as she lightly snored. I dropped my jeans and t-shirt on the floor only wearing my boxers and pulled the covers back gently admiring her naked frame.

I exhaled a long sigh of contentment. The prolonged anticipation of wanting to be back in her arms, and her sweet, warm sex caused my dick to twitch. I crawled in on the side of her body, and slowly glided my hand down her chest, to her stomach, and thigh. Her eyes blinked slowly, but she didn't move.

I leaned over and kissed her shoulder.

"Sweetheart," I whispered, then pressed a kiss behind her ear as she moaned.

"Mmmm... Joaquin," she faintly said with her eyes closed.

"Baby, I want you to come home." I trailed my tongue across her shoulder, down her chest to her nipple.

"Ssss...mmmm," she moaned.

"I miss tasting you."

"Ughhh…" she cried out with her eyes still closed.

"Can I taste you baby?" I asked as I dipped my index finger in her fat, wet sex.

"Arhghh…fuck…Yes, Joaquin." She opened her legs wider.

Her eyes popped open. The sound of her voice affected me deeply, each time I saw her the pull was stronger. My fingers softly caressed her body as I sealed my mouth over hers.

"Mmmmmm…" I groaned and pushed my boxers down lower as her arms wrapped around my neck.

"Yes…Yes…" Sofia cried out as I eased in at a slow pace. I hadn't been with her since before the incident or any woman because no one else could cause this deep longing and feeling of happiness. She folded one leg over my back, and I bent at the knees, with my head back as I thrusted my hips forward.

"Ughhh…fuck," I murmured, grabbing the top of the comforter with my right hand. Beads of sweat popped out on my forehead. Her soft curves molded to the contours of my lean body.

I watched her carefully from the corner of my eyes.

"Joaquin," she called out.

"Shushhh."

I captured her mouth in a slow, affectionate kiss. She clutched at my arms, pulled me in closer as I pushed in deeper.

"Ohhh…God."

"I love you, Sofia. Sweetheart, you're my wife," I said as I dipped my head down to taste her nipples again. I felt a primal ownership now; a deep powerful surge started to explode. My strokes became erratic, as she ground her pelvis against my groin.

"Yeah...Tell me again," she demanded as she ran her long nails up my chest. My knee nudged her legs wider as wetness seeped out and I let out a raw groan as our thrusts became rhythmic. Her pussy squeezed my dick and I had to pull out fast before I came too early and taste her. I was rock hard as I sucked on her clit and the dam of her release broke in a frenzy of need and desire.

"Baby...Joaquin...Ahhh," Sofia cried out.

"Move in with me." I smacked her gently on the ass. She grabbed the tip of my head and ground herself against my tongue.

"Joaquin."

"Move in with me, sweetheart, you'll have this every night." I grazed against her sensitive center as she shivered in my hold. I pushed back inside picked up my pace, drove faster, hearing our groans and cries of pleasure until she came and cried out my name. A second later my dick swelled and I released inside of her feeling worn out and exhausted. I fell on top of her, kissed all over her face and lips.

"Move in with me please, baby."

"Okay," she responded and fell back to sleep. I smirked hearing her snores and fell to the side of the bed and pulled the covers up, wrapping her under my arms. We both had a lot to talk about in the morning and hopefully this wasn't just sex for her. I planned on making her my wife officially with the Fuertes last name.

...

I got up extra early to have breakfast delivered and coffee ready to keep her from running out and avoiding the conversation. I had pancakes, waffles, eggs, fruit, and toast, with juice and oatmeal if she didn't want a big meal.

I showered in the guest room as not to wake her up. I cut the toast in half and grabbed the butter to put on the table.

"Morning," I said as I stared at the most beautiful angel that had a harsh grimace on her face.

"What happened to space, Joaquin?" Sofia mentioned, wearing only my t-shirt that I had left here a few months back.

"You look good in my shirt. I was wondered where I left it."

"Don't change the subject. I want my key back."

"That's fine, let the landlord know you'll give your notice today," I replied as I poured orange juice in a glass, and held it out for her.

"I'm not moving."

"Yes you are," I said.

"Did you find Ciro and Edward?" she questioned.

"I did, but I wanted you to move in even before this happened."

I dropped the spatula, strolled over, and wrapped my arms around her waist.

"Last night you agreed, sweetheart." I kissed the nape of her neck.

"I was in the heat of the moment."

I sighed, pressed my forehead against hers.

"I love you and being apart has only caused problems."

"For me or you?" she asked as she peered up into my eyes.

"Me, I need you and not being able to see you, talk to you is not good for my heart."

"I thought you didn't do love, this was just a fling," she spoke before she stepped out of my hold.

"What are you saying?"

"Are you really in love with me or is this just about in-house pussy?" she probed, took a bite of the toast and sat down.

"If it was just about sex, do you think I would buy a house?"

She choked on the orange juice and I patted her back.

"Hold up, you bought a house? When?"

"It was going to be a surprise during the boat trip, but things went off plan."

"What about kids? We didn't use protection last night," she asked.

"I want children with you."

"Did you kill Edward and Ciro?" she questioned.

"That's something you don't have to worry about."

"For us to move forward I need you to be honest with me."

"I took care of our problems, that's all you need to know."

"Monica?"

"A faded memory." I pushed my chair next to hers and started to fill my plate with food.

"What do your parents think about this?"

"Sweetheart, you ask too many questions," I said, and kissed the top of her nose.

"Where is the house located?" she asked.

"New Jersey in a gated community and you'll have a car driving you around."

"I have to go back on set in a few days with Dante."

"I understand, my men won't cause a problem."

"I haven't agreed to anything yet. This doesn't mean I'm going to fall back into your charms," she spat as she rolled her eyes.

"Would you like some more convincing?" I teased, as I pinched her nipple through the shirt.

"No, you're on probation."

"What!" I shouted and she bent over laughing.

I grabbed her up and carried her to the couch and tickled her stomach and side.

"Okay, okay. I'll move in, but you have to meet with my parents for dinner soon," Sofia explained and I agreed with a kiss.

"My sister wants to hang out. Can you meet with her for lunch or something?" I said while I pushed a piece of hair out of her face.

"I knew she was back and in school, we made plans to have lunch."

"When were you going to tell me?"

"I didn't think I needed to tell you. Everywhere I go your men follow."

"For your protection, baby."

"Is Antonio like this with Sabrina?" she asked.

"Like what?"

"Crazy, possessive, arrogant, bossy," she rattled off.

"Is that your description of me?"

"What would you call it?" she replied as she eased her hands up my chest.

"I would say a man that was so struck by your intelligence, beauty, and confidence that he needed to know everything about her."

"What conclusion did you come up with?"

"Love."

"Love doesn't hurt, Joaquin."

"My love is pure, Sofia, but it can be dangerous when someone hurts what I love."

"Has the Cartel ruined you?"

"How is your music coming along?" I questioned to change the subject.

"I need to set up studio time with Chauncey, mostly been working on modeling for now."

"You're a natural."

"Thank you."

"Let's finish breakfast and then you can tell me all about the music and acting."

"I'm not hungry anymore," Sofia spoke.

"You want to go see the house?" I asked.

She shook her head no and slid her palm further down in my boxers.

CHAPTER 10

Sofia
The intensity in his eyes bore into mine. I reached up to grab his face with my free hand and kiss his lips. Last night, I couldn't fight the pent-up anger inside of me. I can admit I missed him and loved when we just sat around and talked about life. I knew some people would look at him as some thug, but he was everything I wanted and needed. Putting the walls back up and pushing him away would only cause us heartache and living life without the one you loved because of ego and pride was a crutch of a burden. His breath tickled my neck as I felt his first stroke. Dark curly hair smelled like my strawberry shampoo that I kept in the guest shower. His hands slid over my waist, as I clutched at his back.

"Fuck! Sofia."

I teased his mouth as his hands gripped my breasts under my shirt.

"Yess...Ohhh."

"Baby."

My concentration was scattered as his pace picked up

and my belly quivered. Hot tingles were shooting up and down my spine.

"Joaquin, don't stop!" I cried out.

The rush of his kiss, the intensity of his hands all over my body; it was coming too fast and hard. Molding our flesh together was the ultimate spark that gave me a rush of excitement since the first time we made love.

A low groan left his lips.

"Ughhh..."

"I love you, Joaquin," I whimpered as he drove deeper. My climax surged through me as I screamed in ecstasy.

"Ahhhh...I'm coming."

"Fuck! Me too, sweetheart."

"Shittt..." I could feel the tremors of his release as he fell forward and clutched me tighter. He kissed me on the lips and looked down between us. He licked his lips and eased a finger across the head of his base with remnants of our orgasm and brought it to my lips. I stuck my tongue out, he eased his finger in slowly, never taking my eyes off of him as I tasted us together.

"I'm never letting you go again," he spoke.

I knew he was serious this time and by the way he avoided telling me how he killed Edward and Monica, meant Joaquin went off the rails when I wasn't around.

"Kiss me?" I asked, and he bent down like he was about to kiss me and then bit my upper lip.

"Don't ever think this is over, beautiful. Space doesn't exist in my world," Joaquin commented as he gently brushed his tongue around my bottom lip. I glided my hand up around his neck, he smirked as I gently squeezed.

"I know you're crazy, but I can get even crazier, Mr. Fuertes."

...

Two hours later after eating breakfast and going for a second round on the couch and floor, I left Joaquin sleeping in bed and I met up with Alessandra, Sabrina, and Janice at the house Joaquin purchased. I texted Cassidy to meet me there since she'd need to help me with finding an interior designer. Hugo drove across town getting on the highway after picking up Alessandra.

"How are you liking fashion school?" I asked.

"I wish I had done it sooner. Sofia, it's amazing and the people I get to meet," Alessandra rushed out.

"How many classes are you taking?"

"Right now, I'm taking three. Joaquin and my parents want me to be available for family events," Alessandra responded, rolled her eyes.

"What's that look?" I chuckled at her pretending to vomit.

"He doesn't know about me and Gael," Alessandra confessed.

"Oh."

"Exactly."

Hugo stopped at the light, looked through the rearview mirror then sped off into traffic.

"Gael's his best friend, right?"

"Yes, right-hand man. He's like a brother to him."

"That can be tough when you're dealing with two alpha males."

"Can you talk to him for me?" Alessandra begged.

I held my hand up.

"No, I have enough problems with your brother now."

"Please, Sofia, he listens to you," Alessandra pleaded, grasped my hand.

"I'm sorry, Alessandra, you're an adult. Stop acting like a little girl," I said.

"Gael said the same thing."

"He's not happy with being a secret."

She shook her head no.

"No, we've been talking for the past year. I've loved him for the past three years."

"Let me guess, he only saw you as a little sister."

"Yeah." She sighed as she looked out of the window as the car approached a gated area.

"Just be honest, all he can do is say no. You're grown," I said then watched as Hugo typed in the code for the security gate and drove on for another five minutes through a winding road.

"Wow," Alessandra said.

"This place is huge."

"I knew Joaquin had money, but this is insane," Alessandra stated and I nodded in agreement. It had to be more than twenty thousand square feet. It looked to be on its own island.

"Hugo, how much did he pay for this?" I investigated. My mouth dropped open when I opened the door. It was like something out of a fairy tale, the grand sixty-foot marble entrance with double staircase, and a high, probably over thirty feet ceiling. It had a unique hexagon shaped atrium with a two-story colonnade reminiscent of an Italian Palladian Villa. I walked toward what I thought was the kitchen but instead found an impressive thirty-five foot dining room, and a two-story library around the corner. The bar room, media room, and walk-in coat room were ideal for entertaining on a large scale as well as everyday five-star living. I saw a private patio, and the outdoor terraces off the breakfast room which led to the Olympic sized pool.

"I can't believe he did this," I muttered, held my hand to my mouth in shock.

"He loves you." Alessandra approached behind me.

"I...I...don't know what to say."

"Say you'll make me an auntie very soon," Alessandra teased, and I nudged her in the shoulder as we laughed.

"That's not happening anytime soon. I have too much I want to do with my career."

"I understand, it's one of the reasons I want to get out from under my father's thumb."

"I'm moving too, Carlo. You can have the kids because this house is crazy." I heard a loud boisterous mouth. Janice and Sabrina were walking toward us in the backyard.

"Ignore her," Sabrina said.

I chuckled at Janice flipping Sabrina off.

"Pack my bags and ship them here," Janice told me.

"Is she always like this?" I questioned.

"What, new Mommy? Carlo don't get fucked up," Janice spat then hung up the phone in his face.

"You two are hilarious," I said as I gave her a hug.

Her phone started ringing again and she turned it on silent.

"He's going to kick your ass when you get back," Sabrina stated to Janice.

"Carlo don't run me," Janice said.

"Are you sure because last time we talked you wanted to give him another baby?" Sabrina taunted and Janice smirked.

"Don't worry about my man, little girl," Janice said.

"Sabrina and Janice, this is Alessandra, Joaquin's sister," I introduced her and they shook hands.

"What do you do, Alessandra?" Sabrina questioned.

"Shop," Alessandra responded.

"See I like her," Janice said, and pointed at Alessandra.

"She goes to fashion school," I said.

"That's great, I love seeing women taking charge of their careers," Sabrina said.

"Hopefully one day I'll be a famous fashion designer," Alessandra mentioned.

"So what's the plan, Sofia, we've heard some things and know how the media can get them?" Janice asked, standing next to me.

"Honestly, I'm still trying to fit into this world of Joaquin's and not leave mine behind."

"We can most definitely understand that," Janice responded.

I turned and walked back inside of the house as I saw the door open with Hugo letting Cassidy inside.

"After the kidnapping, I just want to forget everything and him."

"Let me guess, he wouldn't let you," Janice answered.

"Not only did he show up at my apartment the next morning where I kicked him out, he also has had his people following me."

"In a weird sense, that means he was giving you space," Janice said.

"How do you guys deal with these men? I can't keep up."

"It took a few years and some kids that distracted them," Sabrina commented.

"I'm a long way from having kids."

"Hey everybody," Cassidy said and waved.

"Thanks for coming on such short notice."

"No worries, I needed to talk to you anyway," Cassidy responded.

"Well, Joaquin bought a house and I agreed to move in with him."

"Wow...Okay are you getting married?" Cassidy questioned.

"No, we talked and are no longer doing the space thing."

"Big Daddy Dick, put that in her life," Janice joked and Alessandra covered her ears and we all laughed as her face closed up in a scowl.

"Ignore Janice, we talked and decided to give our relationship another chance."

"You need a decorator asap," Cassidy said.

"Yes and set up a dinner for my parents and Joaquin," I explained as she took notes.

"Can we go to the mall?" Alessandra asked.

"Mall and then grab some lunch. I have to run through my lines for the show."

"What do you all have a taste for?" Sabrina queried as we walked out of the house and I locked up. I saw Sabrina's blacked out limo with her driver talking to Hugo, and Cassidy's car out front.

"I could go for some lobster," Janice stated.

"We'll do the mall first and then lunch at *High Step*, a new restaurant that opened up and they have everything from fish and barbecue to burgers and Mediterranean.

"Sounds good to me," Alessandra said and followed me to the car.

"Cassidy, do you want to ride with me?" I asked.

"What about my car?" she responded.

"Hugo can get someone to bring it back to the city," I said and Hugo nodded.

"Okay," Cassidy answered.

"Are you all right? You seem a little off."

CHAPTER 11

Sofia

"Nothing a drink won't cure," Cassidy mumbled.

I could tell something was going on with her and having everybody around wasn't the right time to talk. Hugo followed behind Sabrina's driver and pulled back on the road that led back to the main street. I took my phone out and texted Joaquin about the house.

Me: The house is beautiful.

Joaquin: Beautiful house, for a beautiful woman.

Me: Do you realize this house is huge for just the two of us?

Joaquin: Once we have babies, it won't be.

Me: You're talking crazy now.

Joaquin: We have plenty of time to practice.

Me: I bet you had it all planned out.

Joaquin: Do everything with a purpose.

I giggled at his statement and shook my head.

"Is that my brother?" Alessandra asked.

"Yes."

"I could tell by the wide smile on your face," Alessandra said.

"He's crazy, but I love him."

"You calmed the beast. That's a good thing," Alessandra said.

"He's said that in not so many words, that I bring him peace."

"My brother is crazy, but I love him. My father trained him to be a machine," Alessandra advised.

"What do you mean?"

"No emotions, especially love or affection. His only job in life was to take over the Cartel until you came along," Alessandra mentioned. I felt a weird flutter in my chest at her statement.

"Are you saying all he does is go out killing people?" Cassidy queried.

"He's a contracted killer, well mob boss. I thought you knew all of this," Alessandra said.

"I knew some of his work, not the extent of what his father wanted him to become."

"He's leveled out now," Alessandra randomly blurted out like having a contract killer for a brother was a normal thing you tell people.

The car finally stopped in front of the Cherry Hill mall. Hugo helped all three of us step out and I put my shades on to try and cover myself so I could shop without being bothered.

"Where do you want to start first?" Alessandra asked.

"We can try Michael Kors first," I replied as I followed behind her as Janice locked arms with me.

"I know that look, you're feeling overwhelmed. Trust your man," Janice said.

"I do, he told me in not so many terms that he killed two people. One being my manager."

"Send flowers to his mother and keep it moving. If he killed him, it means he hurt you in some way."

"Carlo talks to you about what he does?"

"Some things, but we're not meant to be involved like that, Sofia. Your job is to be that place for him to shed the day away," Janice stated as we stepped on the escalator.

"Am I being too naive to all this?" I responded.

"Sabrina was in your place at one point," Janice told me.

"And now."

"She's a gun toting Donna that will cut your tongue out and financial advisor during the day," Janice nonchalantly said.

"What about you?"

"Oh, I'm crazy in general, this doesn't faze me." Janice laughed and I shook my head.

All of us got off then headed to the Michael Kors store that was up front. I went to the dress section and picked over a few cocktail dresses when a flash bulb went off in my face.

"Sofia, is it true your manager is missing?" a photographer asked.

"Step back," Sabrina said.

"We have every right to be here," the photographer called out as a second one started taking my picture.

"Let's just go," I said, covering my face.

"Edward's family put out a missing person's report," the photographer called out.

"Edward's a grown man. Get out of her face," Janice snapped and pushed them back as we walked out of the store.

"Don't touch me, lady!" he told me.

"Get out of the way," Janice shouted and pushed through the crowd that started to surround us.

"What if I don't, you're going to make me disappear too?" he chuckled, and continued filming us.

"I can make that happen if you want," Janice remarked and Sabrina covered Janice's mouth.

"I guess the day is officially ruined," Alessandra said.

"We'll come back another day." I wrapped my arm around her shoulder and we walked back out to the car.

"I need to head home and start dinner. We can set up another day to have lunch," Sabrina said through the window of our car.

"No worries, sorry about this," I said, and leaned up against the back of the seat.

"One of the things I wanted to talk to you about was the news," Cassidy remarked.

"Edward's disappearance has nothing to do with me or Joaquin."

"I'm not so sure about that," Cassidy said and passed her phone to me with a picture of an SUV in front of a house.

"Whose house is that?"

"Edward's."

"I don't understand."

"This was posted on social media Celebrity Underdark, they say it's Joaquin's car in front of Edward's house."

"Set up an interview, it's time I talked."

"Are you sure?"

"Positive. I can't let this overshadow my career."

...

One Week Later.

I was sitting in front of Jean Shaw of *Morning American* news preparing to answer some questions. Cassidy was here officially as my manager now, until I could hire another publicist. The director wanted to meet with me and the executive producer as soon as possible to talk about everything that was going on. The afternoon we walked out of the mall, photographers followed us back to the city and continued trying to force me into conversation about Edward. I even had a call from the police about coming in to answer some questions. I hadn't said anything about the police to Joaquin yet, my goal was to try to handle what I could without him being thrown in the mix more than he was.

"Miss Chambers thank you so much for joining us today," Jean said as the lights shone down and the mic in her ear was fixed.

"Thank you for giving me the chance to talk about everything."

"America loves you and wants to know how you're doing through these terrible times," Jean said.

"I'm doing better, Jean. As you know I went through something awful and wouldn't wish it on anyone."

"Take us back to that day," Jean said.

"It was another beautiful night in the city. I was meeting with my friend for dinner."

"Your boyfriend, a Mr. Fuertes correct?"

"Yes."

"What happened exactly?"

"I trusted someone that didn't have my best interests."

"The police have mentioned Leonardo was one of the men that took you."

"Leonardo and unfortunately, my ex-manager, Edward."

"This Leonardo person has mob ties to your boyfriend?" Jean questioned.

"My boyfriend has been nothing but supportive

through all of this and the way stories are being written about him have nothing to do with who kidnapped me."

"Are you saying your boyfriend is not a Cartel leader?" Jean asked.

"I'm saying I was taken and almost killed and if it wasn't for my boyfriend and his friends, the outcome might have been far different. Wherever Edward is, I hope the police find him soon and he gets the help that he needs."

"Thank you, Sofia. We understand this is a difficult time for you." Jean leaned over and passed me a tissue. I wiped the tears that pooled in my eyes.

"Extremely, I just want to focus on my career."

"What do you have coming up for the future?"

"More acting and music hopefully soon," I explained.

"Thank you again, Sofia, and America, you've heard it here first from Sofia Chambers on the kidnapping and rescue," Jean said into the camera. The producer called cut and I checked my makeup one more time and shook hands with Jean then strolled to Cassidy.

"What do you think?"

"I think you're a good actress," Cassidy joked.

"I think so too." I laughed and followed behind her out of the building.

"What do we have to do next?" I asked, checking my messages.

"We need to meet with the director and executive producer," Cassidy said.

"That's fine, give Hugo the address," I told her and pulled my mirror out to fix my makeup.

Cassidy leaned over and showed Hugo the address to the studio. Dante told me they were thinking of recasting my part and I was beyond pissed. That role was made for me and we were halfway with filming before the kidnapping happened. Hugo took a right turned on 23rd and Avenue, stopping at Lincoln Studios. I stopped him from getting out. This wasn't that type of visit and having Hugo walking inside with me would have paparazzi roaming around. Cassidy came around to the passenger side and got out. The security guard let us walk through without any issue as I smiled.

I saw Jeremiah talking with Bob Stinger, the executive producer and vice president of the studios.

"Sofia, thanks for coming." Jeremiah extended his hand and I put on a fake smile and reached over to cup his palm.

"Thanks for calling me, Jeremiah."

"We can meet in Bob's office," Jeremiah said.

"How are you doing, Sofia?" Bob asked.

"I'm good, Bob, we just left *Morning America* news."

"That's why we texted Cassidy since you had an interview already and we wanted to catch you early."

"Of course."

"Have a seat," Jeremiah said, and I took the seat on the couch next to Cassidy.

"I know Cassidy probably told you our concerns," Jeremiah started to say.

"She did and I can assure you my personal life won't affect the filming."

"Sofia, you just dealt with a kidnapping and now your manager is missing," Bob said.

"I'm aware, but Cassidy's taking on more responsibility and Edward as you know was involved."

"We've heard rumors your boyfriend is in the mob," Jeremiah stated.

"Rumors."

"Yeah and I know from the one time when he barged in on set trying to fight Dante," Jeremiah reminded me.

"That won't happen again. He can be a little jealous at

times, but we've talked about what my career means to me."

"Can you guarantee he won't interfere if we bring you back on set?" Bob asked.

"Yes."

"How is the investigation going?" Jeremiah questioned.

"I'm not sure, my lawyer handles all of that. Listen, I'm here to work, that's it."

"We understand, but financially we can't take a loss," Bob said.

"Are you saying you'll remove me? The biggest star on this project."

"Try to understand, Sofia. We have to think about the safety of the entire crew and staff," Bob responded.

"I'm telling you everything will be fine; my personal life won't interrupt my business."

"Give us a little time to think it over," Jeremiah told me.

"I'm still in the process of recording my album and I just finished signing a contract to model."

"If the investigation closes we can see about starting back," Jeremiah explained.

"Okay, keep me updated. I don't want to take on another project, but I will," I stated and stood up shaking hands with them both before leaving the room.

"You think they'll call you?" Cassidy asked.

"In three, two, one." Cassidy's phone rang and she answered as I climbed inside of the car.

"Hugo can we drop Cassidy off, then head home?" He motioned in agreement and reversed in the street and headed into traffic.

"Yes, sounds good, Jeremiah. We look forward to working with you as well." Cassidy grinned and hung up, screaming in excitement.

CHAPTER 12

Sofia
The next day.

Joaquin had an intense stare as he watched me hit the stop button on the elevator. I wasn't a prude or anything, but I knew they probably had cameras in the elevator watching us. I switched in front of him slowly and unbuttoned my coat.

"Cover your ears," Joaquin said.

"Why?"

As soon as the words left my mouth, Joaquin lifted his gun and shot at the camera up top as the bell rang.

"OMG!"

"Sweetheart, I warned you to cover your ears," he spoke and reached out and pulled me in close. He locked his eyes with mine and captured my lips as he kneaded my breasts through the shirt. I turned us with his back against the wall and I slid down in front of him and unbuckled his pants. I lingered over the tip in admiration and licked up the head of precum that oozed out. Based on his hissing noises I was driving him crazy. I swirled my tongue over the head and down to the base of his balls as he pushed in my mouth to the hilt. I heard him curse and groan in pleasure.

"Fuck!"

I pulled back and spit on the tip.

"You like that?" I questioned.

"Sofia…" His eyes tensed as I took him back in my mouth.

"Tell me. Do you like this?" I asked and kissed the underside of his balls, while squeezing his dick.

"God damn it!"

"Are you going to fuck me?" I taunted, then watched his head fall back and eyes roll back. I gripped the sides of his thighs and took him back in my mouth as he pumped feverishly. After two more thrusts, his release flowed down my throat. He gently pulled out of my mouth and picked me up and pushed in and I felt a shiver crawl up my spine. Hungrily, he took my mouth at the same time and I snaked my arm around his neck.

"Mmmmm." Desire encompassed me and I felt alive once again. He knew what buttons to push and how to take me to the next level without even trying.

Banging on the door came.

"We'll get you out in one minute," a voice yelled.

"Fuck! Sofia, your pussy drives me insane," Joaquin muttered as he bit the nape of my shoulder.

"Baby, we have to stop…Ahhh…" I screamed in pleasure. My hips rose meeting his thrusts as the ache between my thighs called for more.

"No."

"I'm coming!" I cried out as I convulsed in his arms before he pulled out and sucked on my clit. Five minutes later the doors were open, we both looked disheveled, and I couldn't walk so Joaquin carried me to my apartment.

"You shot the elevator camera," I spoke, leaning my head against his shoulder.

He slid his key inside of my apartment.

"I did."

"Joaquin, we talked about this."

"It's better than shooting a person," he replied. I kissed his lips to shut him up.

"What do you have planned for today?" I asked, as he put me down on the couch.

"I have some unfinished business, and then we can have dinner," Joaquin said.

I bent over and laid my head in his lap.

"Okay, my parents are coming back to town."

He ran his hand across my hair.

"If it'll make you happy, dinner with your parents," Joaquin commented.

"Also, I'm going back to filming."

"I understand," Joaquin stated.

"Do you? The crazy, mob boyfriend can't burst on set anymore."

"I promise, I won't go on set anymore."

"I feel like a shift is happening right."

"I talked to Alessandra and she told me about the photographer at the mall." He bent down and kissed me on the lips.

"The media will always hound me because of my job, but I'm not afraid to be with you."

He grinned, ran a finger over my bottom lip then down my chest and thigh.

"Maybe I can skip my meeting."

"Nope, I need to practice my lines and work on my music."

"When are we moving in the house?"

"I can get Cassidy over here to start packing up this weekend," I replied, lifted my hand to his cheek.

"Good, take my card and buy whatever you need," Joaquin insisted as he pulled his wallet out of his pocket.

"You're giving me your credit card," I said and leaned up to face him.

"You can have that and more if you want." Joaquin pressed a kiss to my forehead.

"Well let me call Cassidy now, and get started. Is there anything you want specifically in the house?"

"There's a basement that I don't want touched," Joaquin answered.

"What's in the basement?"

"I'll use it for my office."

"Joaquin, don't do anything that's going to cause the police to come to our house," I demanded.

"Don't worry, have you spoken with the police?"

"Not yet. I know I didn't tell you sooner, but I thought I could handle things."

"Never keep anything from me, Sofia," Joaquin said, standing up.

"Are you going to kill Ciro?"

"Yes," Joaquin answered.

"I want to be there."

"I can't involve you in that, Sofia."

"If we're going to do this, I want to see what you do."

"The second you see me in that environment, you may not stay with me."

"I know what you do. I'm not stupid and I can handle it so let me get changed."

"No, you're not coming." Joaquin followed behind me to the bedroom.

"Sabrina and Janice have seen what Antonio and Carlo do," I argued as I removed my jacket and skirt. I kicked off my heels then opened the closet to grab a pair of jeans and a t-shirt.

He tried to grab the jeans out of my hands.

"Sofia, you're not Sabrina and Janice."

"You think I'm some weak, naive, and fragile girl."

"No, but the less you know about that side of me the better."

I turned and reached my arms around his neck.

"Joaquin, stop treating me like some fragile doll that can't handle herself." I kissed the side of his mouth.

"Are you trying to seduce me?" he asked.

"Only if it's working."

"You still can't come," he said.

"Okay," I replied.

"Good, so order our favorite for dinner and I'll be back soon."

"Sure."

I watched him walk out of the bedroom and leave. I went to my house phone and called the one person I knew that could help me.

"Hello," Janice said.

"Janice, I need your help." I sat on the edge of the bed, unsnapped my bra with the phone between my shoulder and neck.

"What's wrong?" Janice queried.

"Joaquin has Ciro and he's going to kill him."

"That's good right?"

"Yes, but he won't let me be there to watch."

"Just like Antonio and Carlo," Janice remarked.

"So, they treated you guys the same."

"Yep. Antonio tried to run the same thing on Sabrina."

"So can you help me? Find out where they are?" I questioned.

"Yeah, give me about fifteen minutes to get the kids situated."

"Thanks, Janice, I appreciate this," I said and ended the call.

I jumped up and ran to the bathroom to shower and change. I needed to hurry up and get back before Joaquin noticed I was gone for too long. Fifteen minutes later I walked out of the back and picked up my purse and cell phone to call Cassidy. The door buzzed and I checked the monitor to see Janice and Sabrina downstairs.

"Hey, Sofia, I was getting ready to send you an email with the script."

"Thanks, Cassidy."

"Sure, anything else you need?"

"Get tickets for my parents to fly out for me," I said as I walked out of the apartment and took the stairs toward the back exit.

"The police said they wanted to meet with you asap." I pushed the door open of the exit and ran to the side of the wall and waved for Janice to reverse so I could jump in without Hugo noticing me.

"I'll take care of them tomorrow," I responded then ended the call.

"Janice, you didn't say anything about doing something behind Antonio's back," Sabrina fussed, her arms folded across her chest.

"Hurry up, Sofia," she whispered as I slid in and shut the door.

"Sabrina, blame me, I wanted to find out where Ciro was being held," I told her.

"Sabrina, shut up, you act like you've never killed some-one," Janice spat, and waved her off.

"Wait what?"

"We both have done some things...She's the last person

to be shocked," Janice joked as she drove off into traffic.

"How long ago did he leave?" Janice asked.

"About fifteen minutes."

"I have an idea," Janice said.

"You know where they are?' I asked.

"Antonio still has a warehouse on London off Sixth Street," Sabrina said.

"That's true, because the other one was burnt down after killing the DEA agent boyfriend," Janice remarked.

"He killed a DEA agent?" I asked, in shock.

"Among other things," Sabrina replied.

"Pass me my bag back there," Janice said and I picked it up off the floor.

"Here you go."

"You'll need this," Janice said and passed me a gun.

"I don't need a gun."

"Listen if we do this, you have to be all in or we turn back around," Janice said.

"She's right, Sofia. When you agreed to be with him, this is what happens," Sabrina stated.

I grabbed the gun from Janice and checked the safety.

"You only need protection," Janice said.

"Joaquin's going to kill me."

"He'll be upset for a few days, but put the pussy on him and he'll forget being mad," Janice advised, and winked through the rearview mirror.

"Is she always like this?" I asked and Sabrina nodded in answer.

"We're here, ladies," Janice stated before she turned the lights off as we approached the side street of what looked like an empty building.

"This street looks abandoned," I said, looking out of the window at all the lights out. It was around nine at night. A ghost town with nothing but empty buildings around.

Janice pulled a black ski mask down on her face.

"Janice is that necessary?" Sabrina questioned.

"My husband thinks I'm out grocery shopping," Janice replied as I giggled at the two of them arguing back and forth.

"Ignore her, Sofia."

"Where should we start?" I questioned.

"Take the back and see if we can get in," Janice stated, and turned to lead us to the back. The building didn't have any security out front. Janice looked around the corner and pushed us to go back further.

"One guy standing outside," Janice spoke, her voice quiet.

"What do you want to do?" I questioned.

She pulled her gun out, removed the safety.

"Ready?" Janice asked us.

"Are we seriously doing this?" I inquired.

"This is what happens when you date a Cartel boss," Janice explained and put the gun to her side.

"If you want to go home tonight I suggest you give me that gun, big fella," Janice announced, and he chuckled.

"Bitch, you better kill me or else," the guy said.

"Is that any way to talk to Antonio's De Luca's wife?" Sabrina asked.

"Wait," he said and Sabrina hit him over the head with the back of her gun.

"Let's go," Janice whispered and eased the door open, before she glanced around the room. The back room was old and musty with wires hanging off from the ceilings. Janice walked over to the door and peeked inside.

"Fuck! Carlo's here," Janice whispered.

"Which means Antonio is here," Sabrina said as she wiped a hand down her face.

"Did you see Ciro?"

"He's tied up," Janice responded.

"What angle?" Sabrina asked.

"Literally tied up hanging up from the wall." Janice chuckled.

"Move back, Janice, you're gun happy," Sabrina stated and pushed her to the side.

"Okay, it's your show, Sofia, how do you want to do this?" Janice questioned.

"I want to see him."

"Then lead the way," Janice said and I swallowed the lump in my throat.

I opened the door and all heads turned toward me. Joaquin was wearing all black with blood running down his face and clothes.

"I knew this would happen," Carlo said, and threw his hands up in the air.

"Hey husband," Janice responded, putting the gun behind her back.

"You can take the mask off now," Carlo said.

"Sabrina, I thought you were getting the kids in bed," Antonio stated before he walked up to her and pressed a kiss to her lips.

"Blame Janice."

Janice removed her mask.

"Sofia wanted to be here and she deserves to see this scum get what's coming to him," Janice explained and Joaquin's eyes narrowed in anger.

"I'm not leaving," I said to him.

"She needs to see this," Sabrina said.

Ciro laughed as blood spilled from his lips.

"That little bitch would have made a good pet for me," Ciro muttered, in slow breaths.

Joaquin punched him in the face.

"What was the plan, Ciro?" Antonio asked.

"Kill the bitch like he killed my niece," Ciro shouted.

"Edward," I said.

"He wasn't nothing but a patsy. Motherfucker thought he was going to get rich," Ciro stated.

"You need to leave, Sofia," Joaquin said and picked up an automatic screwdriver.

"No, we do this together," I said and pulled out my gun and aimed at Ciro.

"Once you do this, it can't be undone," Joaquin remarked and I knew what he was saying about taking someone's life. I needed to see this piece of shit die, because he might try and come back if he gets away.

I raised the gun up.

"Ready," Joaquin said.

"Fucking bitch!" Ciro screamed as Joaquin drilled into his left knee.

Pop! Pop!

"Ahhhhh!!" Ciro cried out as the bullets went into his chest.

I aimed and focused on his head with one eye closed and let go.

Pop! Pop!

"That's my friend," Janice called out as the bullets went straight to his head and neck.

Joaquin took the gun from me as I started shaking. He lifted my chin, peered in my eyes as tears started to spill down my face.

"You did good," Joaquin said.

"I just killed him."

"Better him than you," Joaquin replied and pulled me in close then kissed my cheek.

He rubbed my back and led me out of the warehouse as his men started to get rid of his body.

CHAPTER 13

*J*oaquin
A week earlier.

WE'D HELD Ciro in captivity for the past week with only water keeping him alive. My men caught him as he left the hotel to try and check out and fly back to Italy.

They followed him on the highway toward the airport and rammed his car. I took the gun out of the back of my waistband and got out of the car and eased the door open.

"You think this is over," Ciro said as my men dragged him out of the car.

"Only the beginning."

"Fuck you!" Ciro said and I punched him in the face.

"Take him to the car."

"Your little girlfriend still isn't safe," Ciro taunted.

"What did you say?"

"Joaquin, we can't stay out here. He's fucking with you," Gael advised.

Hugo and Gael dragged Ciro to the car.

"Motherfucker needs to die," I shouted, and hit the top of the car.

"We have to go, Joaquin, before his people get word," Gael yelled and I hopped in the van as Gael drove off running a red light.

"Call Antonio," Gael said as my phone vibrated.

"We got him," I spoke into the phone.

"Bring him to the warehouse," Antonio commanded, ending the call. I balled my fist up ready to kill him with my bare hands.

"He had his slimy hands on her."

"I hear you, but we need to do it in a place that won't attract police."

"Sofia's going back to work and I want this finished before it happens."

"We'll handle it," Gael said.

PRESENT DAY.

"Ughh...Joaquin," Sofia moaned, as I punished her with a smack to her ass, her cries were muffled in the sheets. As soon as we left out of killing Ciro I drove us home and ripped her clothes off and massaged her clit with my finger and tongue. The kiss to the back of her neck was slow and soothing as my warm body hovered over hers, as my hands landed on her full breasts and gently tweaked her nipples. The soft moan out of her echoed through the room. My hips slowly rotated as I focused on her breathless whimpers. Sofia fell down on top of the bed, and I closed her legs with my dick still inside as her pleasure intensified and I growled as my body trembled as her essence poured out. I leaned further on down, whispered in her ear about how much I loved her and needed her in my life.

"Sweetheart..." I grunted, reached underneath us and massaged her clit with my thumb.

"Keep going...Mmmmm."

"Shit...baby." I plunged deeper, succumbed to her trembles as I jerked in the explosion. I fell on my side and lifted her left leg and pushed back inside.

"Don't stop!" she screamed as she reached around to grab the back of my head.

"I'm coming, baby," I said, as her opening clenched and milked me of every drop. My hips pushed in rapid succession.

"Yessss...Oh God!" Sofia cried out, as her mouth crashed onto my lips as we drunkenly fell deeper in love.

My eyes started to close, and I pulled her in my arms. An hour later I ordered dinner as she slept and I put everything on a plate with a glass of wine. I showered and threw on my boxers and came back into the bedroom and she was awake, surprisingly watching tv.

"Hey," Sofia said.

"Hungry?"

"Starving." She took the glasses of wine off the tray and put them on the nightstand. I put the tray down in front of us on the edge of the bed. I moved the covers over and laid down next to her as she grabbed the rice and orange chicken bowl.

"Was that Ghost I saw tonight?" she asked.

"A small piece of him."

"Janice said something interesting to me about how we need to be your escape," she spoke.

"I didn't want you to lose yourself in what I do."

"I'm okay, Joaquin."

"The second you feel you're not."

"I don't look at you differently, I appreciate how you take care of me," she replied.

"Even when I get controlling?" I fed her a piece of my egg roll.

"Hopefully now you'll step back a little."

"That won't happen," I joked and bit her arm gently.

"What happened to Ciro's body?"

"You really want to know?"

"Yes."

"I put his body in acid."

"What about Edward?"

"I chopped him up," I confessed.

"Wow."

"Does that scare you?"

"I need to go to talk to the police tomorrow," Sofia said.

"I'll send my lawyer with you."

She took a sip of the wine.

"They'll probably ask me about Edward's disappearance."

"You don't know anything about his life and what he did outside of managing your career."

"Let's go to bed, I'm exhausted." She yawned and drank the last of her wine. I took the bowls and put them on top of the tray and put it all on top of the dresser. I pulled the covers up, sighed and wrapped her in my arms.

…

The morning came and Sofia was out of the door with Cassidy and I called my lawyer to meet her at the police station. I had a few calls to make and business at Alba Industries until we had dinner tonight. I checked my wallet and tie, grabbed my keys and walked out of her apartment and headed down to the awaiting car. I hopped in the back of the car with Gael.

"Where to?" Gael asked.

"I want to check on Alba Industries and get Mauricio on the phone."

"We need to talk about something," Gael stated.

"What?" I asked.

"I didn't want it to be like this, but I'm dating Alessandra," Gael said.

"How long has this gone on?" I asked as Gael stopped at the stop sign.

He sighed and ran his hand down his face.

"About a year."

"I already knew."

"What do you think your father will say?" Gael questioned.

"He'll probably want you killed," I joked.

"Fuck you," Gael said.

I ran a hand through my beard.

"You dating my sister isn't my favorite thing."

"But." Gael glanced at me in the passenger seat.

I shrugged my shoulders.

"We've known each other all of our lives. You hurt her."

"You kill me," Gael responded.

"We understand each other."

"We do," Gael said.

Gael parked in his reserved space at Alba Industries. We stepped out, and I buttoned my jacket before I made sure my gun was still safe and secure. I nodded at the security guard and valet as I walked into the building and smiled at the receptionist. Gael went over to check with security as I continued onto the elevator and headed to my office. A few minutes later I grabbed messages from my assistant and opened the door to my office then checked leftover voice messages.

"Sir, are you going to be here for lunch today?" my assistant asked.

I checked my watch. It was going on nine am, and

normally lunch was at a restaurant if I was meeting with a new client.

"For now order from Bar One and have it delivered," I replied.

"Yes, sir."

I turned my computer on, checked emails and saw two prospective clients wanting to meet about investing in their companies. I responded to both, requesting that they send over a portfolio of their latest numbers and board members.

"Mauricio just messaged to call him."

"What does he want?" I questioned and dialed his number on my cell phone and put it on speaker.

"Joaquin," Mauricio said.

"What can I do for you, Mauricio?"

"Laurent was informed about Ciro," Mauricio stated.

"I don't know what you're talking about."

He chuckled.

"Is this how you do business over a woman?" he spat.

"This is how I do business, Mauricio, does Laurent have concerns?"

Gael took his phone out and dialed a number.

"I'm speaking on behalf of Carrington Cartel. Ciro was a big buyer for us," Mauricio remarked.

"Sorry to tell you, but he will no longer be a buyer."

"Do you think this woman is worth you losing money?" Mauricio stated.

"Mauricio, we do business, don't worry about my personal life."

"The pussy must be really good," he said.

I slammed my hand down on the desk and cursed in Portuguese.

"If you want to continue doing business with me, then you'll never speak those words again."

"You don't scare me, Joaquin. I'm the next underboss," Mauricio said.

"Would you like to meet Ghost?"

"I just want you to remember money is not worth a woman," Mauricio mentioned.

"I'll take that into consideration for next time," I said and hung up.

Gael ended his call.

"That was Laurent."

"What did he say?" I asked.

"He didn't know Mauricio was calling you," Gael commented, sitting down in front of my desk.

"What do you think the angle is?" I twisted my phone in my hand and stared at the ceiling.

"He could be trying to take over Laurent's seat."

"That motherfucker," I said.

"He's moving funny," Gael responded.

"Hugo's with Sofia right now, make sure the house has extra security," I said. Gael left to go meet up with Alessandra and I told him about reminding her about dinner with Sofia's family tonight.

Me: How is it going?

Sofia: We just pulled up.

Me: My lawyer should be inside waiting for you.

Sofia: I know, he messaged he would meet us.

Me: Tell him to call me right after.

Sofia: I will.

Me: If they get disrespectful, let me know.

Sofia: I don't need you doing anything to the police.

I smirked at her text.

Me: Baby, don't worry. The police can't touch me.

Sofia: They just came out to get me.

Me: Okay, keep me updated as soon as you're done.

Sofia: Love you.

Me: Love you more.

I closed out of the messages and continued working for the rest of the day on my legit businesses.

"Mr. Fuertes, your sister's on the phone," the assistant said.

"Thanks," I replied, and picked up my office phone.

"Gael told you," Alessandra said.

"He did."

"Are you mad?" Alessandra asked.

"I'm disappointed you didn't tell me, but if you're happy, that's what's important."

"I wasn't trying to keep it secret, we just happened," Alessandra spoke.

"Alessandra, I don't believe you for one second, but it's your life."

"Fine, but can you be there when I tell father?" Alessandra asked.

"I have dinner with Sofia's parents tonight, I'll call you when my schedule clears," I replied and hung up. The only thing on my mind was how Sofia was doing at the police station.

CHAPTER 14

Sofia

I slid my phone in my purse, squared my shoulders and looked forward not showing any type of emotion that would cause the police to think I was intimidated by them. I already felt they were trying to set me up or put my name in a bad light because when we pulled up the paparazzi were outside and I know I didn't call them down here. The only people that knew we'd be here were the officers working on Edward's case, Cassidy, and myself.

"Miss Chambers thank you for joining us today," Detective Jones said.

"Of course," I replied.

Joaquin's lawyer, Emilio, motioned for me to take a seat next to him.

"You didn't need a lawyer with you, we're just asking routine questions," Detective Adams spoke with a silly grin on his face. I didn't like him at all because he seemed like he was on another agenda separate from finding what happened to Edward. I was surprised he had a wedding ring on his hand with the way he came across and smelled. He had a large belly that looped over his pants, a bald head, and was sweating profusely with a tooth missing at the bottom right corner; he just gave off a creepy vibe.

"Let's get on with this, Detective," Emilio said.

"When was the last time you saw Edward?" Detective Jones asked while he pulled out a notepad and pen.

"The last time I saw him was before my kidnapping."

"You haven't spoken to him for over two months," Detective Adams said.

"Yes."

"You don't think that's strange?" Detective Adams responded.

"No, Edward and I weren't close friends."

"Where do you think he'd go?" Detective Jones said.

"I don't know," I responded as I crossed my arms over my chest and leaned back in the chair.

"She's lying," Detective Adams spat.

"Watch it, Detective," Emilio said.

"We know Edward was in love with you, Sofia...Are you telling us that he just up and left?" Detective Jones stated.

"I'm not telling you anything...the last time we spoke it was about business."

"I think your boyfriend killed him," Detective Adams said.

"That's crossing the line, Adams," Emilio spoke.

"I'm wondering why his lawyer is down here," Adams remarked.

"My client doesn't have to explain to you who she hired," Emilio insisted.

"He has you wrapped around his finger. The pussy must be good," Detective Adams said.

"Detective! I want him removed," Emilio shouted.

"It's okay, Emilio," I said.

He grinned.

"Edward, like all men, has tried and failed to get me to sleep with them."

"You don't need to explain this," Emilio muttered.

"No, he needs to understand."

"Understand what? That some rich bitch thinks she can waltz in here?" Detective Adams sneered.

"Adams," Jones commented.

"No, let him keep going and see what happens."

"Are you threatening me?" Adams asked, hovering over the table.

I laughed, seeing him turn red.

"I don't need to threaten anyone, Detective, I didn't do anything wrong."

"Then give us a DNA sample and tell us what happened to Edward," Detective Jones stated.

"This questioning is going to be over before it really starts," Emilio said.

"I had nothing to do with Edward missing."

"Then your boyfriend knows something," Detective Jones implied as he pushed a photo of Edward and Ciro talking together in front of a hotel.

"Who is that?" I questioned, pointing at Ciro.

"This is the man that took you. Do you know him?" Detective Jones asked.

"This was the first time seeing him. Well besides the kidnapping," I spoke.

"Ciro Vitale is a powerful man in the Cartel world, the entire family is almost wiped out," Jones said.

"Sorry to hear that."

"Because of your boyfriend," Adams shouted.

"That's it, get him out of here," Emilio said.

"Fine, I'll let you handle it." Jones took a sip of his coffee.

"Ciro came here looking for Joaquin about his niece's death," Jones said.

"I don't know anything about that, I was almost killed on that boat."

"And somehow you're here without a scratch on you," Adams said.

"Detective Adams is this personal to you?" I asked.

"Nothing is personal to me," Adams said.

"It has to be, I mean, you're so hard up about Joaquin."

"The guy you're in love with is evil, he's killed people," Jones stated.

"Joaquin Fuertes is a business owner."

"Is that what you're going with?" Jones asked.

"That's what I know."

"This is over," Emilio said as he grabbed his briefcase and stood up.

I clasped my purse and jumped up and started to follow him.

"He's not a good man, Miss Chambers. Think of your family," Jones said.

I stopped at the door with my hand on the wall.

"Are you threatening me?" I questioned over my shoulder.

"It's a suggestion," Adams commented.

I smirked, pinned a piece of my hair behind my ear and turned to look at them both.

"I'll let Joaquin know about your suggestions. Good day, detectives," I spoke and walked out of the room.

"Don't worry about them, they don't have anything on you," Emilio said as he held the door open letting me out first. I saw Hugo and Cassidy standing in front of the car waiting on us.

"I know."

"Tell Joaquin I'll be in contact."

"Thank you, Emilio."

"Anytime and I'm a big fan of your work, Miss Chambers."

I reached out and shook hands with him.

"Thank you and don't take this personally, but I hope to not use your services again."

"Joaquin will have an update by the time you get home and things will be rectified," Emilio stated, waved through the window.

I climbed in the backseat of the car as Hugo shut the door.

"How did it go?" Cassidy asked.

"It's not something that I enjoyed, but I told the truth," I said.

"Well at least it's behind you now," Cassidy muttered.

I sighed, looked out of the window in thought.

"You have to be on set tomorrow don't forget," Cassidy reminded me.

"I won't and I need to stop at the grocery store for food. My parents fly in tonight."

"Dinner with the parents," Cassidy advised.

"Yep."

"Good luck, I can't see Joaquin being nervous to convince your parents to like him," Cassidy joked.

"Me neither, so more than likely it'll turn into an argument."

"What about his parents?" Cassidy remarked.

"I met them a while back and his mom loves me."

"His father?" she questioned.

"It was touch and go at first, but now we seem to be fine."

"Joaquin doesn't look like the type to allow anyone to tell him what to do," Cassidy stated.

"He's not. Well besides me." I giggled.

I slid my vibrating phone out and saw a message from Joaquin.

Joaquin: I talked to Emilio.

Me: That didn't take long.

Joaquin: I pay him well.

Me: Detectives didn't have real evidence.

Joaquin: Did they threaten you?

Me: In a non-sort of threatening tone.

Joaquin: Ciro had them on payroll.

Me: So you think they're trying to set me up?

Joaquin: They're not stupid enough to do that.

Me: I'm almost home, will talk later.

Hugo turned in front of Cassidy's apartment building and waved goodbye as she got out to leave.

"Hugo, can you run me by the store and then home?" I asked. He nodded in answer and we headed up the street to the store.

...

An hour later I was sauteing vegetables, while the steaks cooked on the stove. I opened a bottle of red wine and put another one in the fridge to chill. Joaquin was on his way with his sister and my parents were getting picked up by Hugo from the airport. I made sure to have something for everybody tonight. My parents were still hesitant about us and I wanted them to see that I was fine and protected not only with my heart, but my safety thanks to Joaquin.

Beep!

The buzzer sounded and I dropped the utensils and wiped my hands on the towel and walked to the door.

"Yes."

"Hey, sweetie, it's your mom and dad."

"Finally, come on up." I let them upstairs and opened the door to go back to the stove and check on my food before it burned.

"What smells good in here?" Mom called out as she removed her jacket.

"Steak, lasagna, garlic bread," I said.

Mom kissed me on the cheek.

"Hi, Dad."

"Hi, pumpkin, how are you feeling?" he asked, hanging my mom's jacket up.

Before I answered, the door opened further and Joaquin and Alessandra strolled in together.

"You're right on time," I said as he wrapped an arm around my waist and kissed my cheek.

"I brought some more wine," Joaquin explained.

"Perfect."

"Mr. and Mrs. Chambers." Joaquin extended his hand to my father and I held my breath waiting to see if an argument would start.

"Joaquin," Father responded and reached out to shake his.

"Hello, I'm Alessandra, Joaquin's sister," she said.

"Hi Alessandra, you're gorgeous. Are you a supermodel?" Mom questioned.

CHAPTER 15

Sofia

I sprinkled salt and pepper on top of the rice and vegetables, tossed them in the pan and drained the excess grease and poured the concoction over the rice and plated it all into my best dish. I passed Alessandra the garlic bread and vegetables to put on the table.

"Joaquin, I'm not going to sugarcoat this. Why are you with my daughter?" my father blurted out.

"Your daughter is amazing, and I love everything about her."

I stayed quiet as my father grilled him.

"She's our baby. For her to get kidnapped on your watch doesn't sit well with us," Mom spoke.

"I understand. But let me make this clear, Sofia will never be in that situation again," Joaquin said.

"My brother can be an ass, Mr. and Mrs. Chambers," Alessandra said and I giggled.

"Sofia," Mom chastised.

"Sorry."

"He's old school about the way men should be protective over their women."

"Alessandra, our daughter was kidnapped and the police said it was because of your brother," Mom explained.

"The police were trying to scare you," Joaquin said.

"Ma, they will say anything to get me to turn against Joaquin," I said, putting the plate of lasagna on the table. Joaquin pulled me into his arms.

"Do you love our daughter?" Father questioned.

Joaquin stared into my eyes.

"She's my soul," Joaquin replied.

"We can't say who she could be with, our baby is grown. But your job is to protect her," Father stated.

"He's done that. He bought a house for us."

"You're moving in together?" Mom asked.

"Yeah."

"I hope a ring is coming?" Father narrowed his eyes in Joaquin's direction and I felt embarrassed.

"Can we focus on one thing for right now?" I asked.

"I consider her my wife now, but marriage is the next step."

"Joaquin why didn't you tell me?" Alessandra asked, offended.

"Because I knew you'd tell her if I did bring it up," he joked.

"What do you do for work?" Father inquired.

"Business," we both answered at the same time.

"If you're happy then we'll leave it alone," Mom told me.

"Thank you and I am."

"That's all that matters," Mom spoke.

"Can we talk about my boyfriend problems?" Alessandra questioned.

"No," Joaquin responded so I slapped his shoulder.

"Stop acting like that."

"I'm fine with her dating my best friend, but don't want to hear about it," Joaquin informed me.

"He's such an asshole," Alessanda mumbled, as Joaquin buried his face in my neck.

"Let's eat," I said, before he could go further.

He groaned and let me up out of his lap to take a seat next to him.

We laughed and talked with my parents and his sister all night, then Hugo drove them back to the hotel and Alessandra to her condo.

...

"Fuck!" Joaquin shouted, as I sat with my back to him and bounced with both feet flat on top of the bed.

"Mmmm…"

"Ughhhh…fuck you're so beautiful," Joaquin spoke as he smacked my ass.

"Tell me you love me."

"I love you!" Joaquin bellowed as I jumped off and sucked him into my mouth and massaged his balls. I wanted to show him my gratitude for all he'd done for keeping me safe, trusting me with the other side of his world and not letting the darkness keep him away from loving me purely.

CHAPTER 16

 ofia

THE NEXT DAY.

EARLY MORNING CALL time was not my idea of getting back to work after a long night talking with my parents. Then Joaquin keeping me up all night long as he tried rearranging my insides. I had a crick in my neck now after doing new tricks to keep up with him. All I heard was him cursing at me which I could only understand a little with his accent. I learned since we'd been together that when he really gets upset, his accent comes out more. In his mind I shouldn't have known these different moves and he kept asking who taught me. I wouldn't dare tell him; I liked to keep a few secrets to myself.

"So today, what are we doing?" Tonya asked.

"Not too heavy on the foundation today. It's a small scene we're doing."

"Okay are you glad to be back on set?"

"I am, even though it was touch and go with Jeremiah and Bob."

"Yeah, I heard there were rumors of replacing you," Tonya mentioned.

"Cassidy and I had to meet with them."

"I'm glad you're back, how does your boyfriend feel about things?" Tonya questioned, placing a primer on first.

"He won't be showing back up here anytime soon. We have an agreement." I laughed, thinking about me giving Joaquin an ultimatum.

"That man is crazy about you," Tonya said.

"I know."

"What did the police say? It was in the blogs about you talking with them."

"Basic questions about Edward's and my relationship."

"I heard his family filed a missing person's report," Tonya remarked.

"Good, and I hope they find him," I spoke, taking a sip of the water and reading my lines.

"Did he really work with that guy to kidnap you?"

"Unfortunately, that's what they said."

"Wow."

A knock at my trailer interrupted us.

"Come in!" I yelled.

"It's me," Cassidy said, sipping on a smoothie.

"You look cute."

"Thanks, here's your usual, celery juice."

"Thanks," I said and took a sip.

"I thought you weren't showing up until later."

"I wasn't, but I wanted you to see the numbers from clothing sales," Cassidy stated.

"I forgot you launched that sportswear line," Tonya said.

"Expressive Designs. Let me know your size and I'll get Maggie to send some pieces over," I replied.

"The social media awareness is growing and since launch we've hit fifty million in US sales alone, and twenty-five million global," Cassidy stated, scrolling through her phone.

"I liked the black pants and sports bra, maybe a custom set," I said.

"I'll talk to Maggie, but she's happy with the sales and wants to extend the contract," Cassidy told me.

"Good, did you hear from Chauncey about the songs?" I questioned.

"Yep, all set for whenever you're ready to go back in the studio."

"Girl you're crazy busy." Tonya pinned my hair up into a bun.

"If I want to continue on my career path, I have to work ten times harder," I remarked.

"Jeremiah's ready for you," a PA for the show called through the walkie that sat on my vanity mirror.

"Show time," I said and removed the cape and stood up. I wore the detective uniform of my character and checked myself out one more time in the mirror before heading out to the set.

"Let them know Sofia Chamber never left," Cassidy gassed me up.

"Thanks, girl."

I stepped out of the trailer and hopped on the golf cart and went to the soundstage to start my day with Dante and hopefully complete filming before I had to start the moving process and finish my album.

...

"Joaquin!" I squeezed my eyes tight as sweat flowed down my stomach. I felt him all the way in my throat, and I was ready to pass out from his powerful thrusts. I knew he missed me since I was out working late. With us both having busy lives, I needed to figure out a balance of everything I had going on with making sure we were still a priority. I planned on finally getting help with packing to move. Now that my parents were on board and respected our relationship, we could move forward with the next steps. Once recording was halfway started and since filming would be done soon the next obstacle was moving. We reconnected all night into the morning. I wanted to get up early and cook his breakfast, but from the moans and grunts, eating food was the last thing on his mind.

Joaquin

I was picking Sofia up from her place tonight, I tried to get her to spend the night, but she wanted to still feel independent. Even though I offered to move her into my building for security reasons, she still argued about needing her own space. Once her parents came around to our relationship things started to calm down and now that my sister was here to live, she became close friends with Sofia. I still wasn't too fond of her dating Gael, but I couldn't do anything besides threaten to kill him if he hurt her. I looked through the rearview mirror and saw Hugo and Gabriella following behind me as a precaution. Ciro was no longer a factor in our lives, but I wasn't naive enough to think it wouldn't cause a ripple effect down the road. Collaborating with Edward to hurt the most important person in my life was the biggest mistake they could have done. I made myself clear when I first saw Sofia and told him that she belonged to me, he should have bowed out gracefully and now his grandmother had to mourn his death. I turned right at the light, near Avalon Clinton apartments and stopped in front of her apartment prepared to head inside and I saw she was already outside waiting with the doorman. She pointed toward the car and the doorman strolled behind her to the door. I wanted to say something about her coming down with her bodyguard, but I let it go for now. Tonight she was all mine and I planned on keeping her all tied up. She got inside the car, placed her hand on my thigh and I smiled.

"How was your day?" I questioned as I turned the signal on to head into traffic.

"It was busy because I had a photoshoot for my album cover."

"When does it come out again?" I stopped behind a red pickup truck that had a baby on board sticker.

I pointed at the sticker.

"Can you see yourself like that one day?"

"Like what?"

"Giving me a child."

"Once my career slows down, I can see us with kids one day."

The light changed and I pulled into traffic. I sighed thinking about her answer.

"Sofia and what about marriage?" I peered at her out of the corner of my eye.

"You think your parents will be okay with marriage?" She fidgeted with her hands.

"No one has a say in what we do, but the two people in the relationship."

"Glad to hear that," she responded, looking out of the window.

"Are you excited for tonight?"

"I'm a little nervous, but excited at the same time. A listening party is huge." She reached over and grabbed my hand, entwining our fingers. We arrived at Ryde nightclub and I got out of the car and walked around to help her step out. I reserved the place with her family, friends, and a few industry people that she worked with to help celebrate her music. Normally I stay out of the public picture, but I wanted to show her my support and arranging this with Cassidy let her know that I'm hundred percent behind her career. The outside door had a huge sign about tonight and a few fans wanted a picture with her, so I let them take them as I turned my back so as not to be seen. She kissed my cheek and signed a few autographs and we strolled in together where we saw a few of her castmates from the Broadway show dancing.

"We have the section in VIP reserved," Cassidy shouted in my ear. I held my hand on Sofia's lower back. Hugo was behind us and Gael in front.

"You want anything to drink?" I asked her.

She shook her head no.

"Just you is all I need." She cupped my face and stood on her tip toes to kiss me.

"Anything for you."

"Is your sister here?" she asked.

"Gael is here, so probably," I responded, and we walked through the crowd and took a seat in the corner. A bottle girl came over and dropped more glasses off.

"I invited Tonya and your parents," Cassidy said.

"I see her now. My parents are probably asleep in bed by now," I heard Sofia reply.

"We're having dinner with my parents tomorrow," I mentioned to Gael and watched as he gulped on his shot of whiskey.

"Your sister told me," Gael stated as he put his arm around my sister's waist and pulled her back down to the couch.

"I was just dancing," Alessandra said, annoyed.

"In a little ass dress," Gael growled out. I didn't blame him; I wouldn't want Sofia in something so damn tiny.

Alessandra rolled her eyes.

"Joaquin, talk to your friend," Alessandra said.

"I told you, I wasn't getting involved in your relationship."

"Stop going to your brother when I say something you don't like," Gael complained.

I chuckled at the pout on her face.

"Baby, come dance with me," Sofia said.

"Sweetheart, I don't dance, I'll watch you though." I pinched her cheek.

"You're no fun," she said, so I pulled her into a searing kiss.

"Ewwweee, get a room," Alessandra fussed.

"You're trying to start something, Mr. Fuertes," Sofia said before she wiped the lipstick off my lips.

"Is it working?" I replied.

She grinned.

"Maybe, but we have at least another hour. So you'll have to wait," she commented and I groaned before I adjusted myself and tried to think of anything other than sex to get my dick to go down. She was looking too sexy and I couldn't go a day without being inside of her and hearing her soft moans. We ended up partying until the club shut down and I took her back to the house and we made love in each room christening it listening to her music play over the radio.

CHAPTER 18

*S*ofia
Three months later.

Today I planned a dinner with my parents and Joaquin's, along with his sister and Gael. The cat was out of the bag with them dating and her father stopped trying to keep them apart after Alessandra threatened to run away. Their mother was adamant about him letting it go and allowing the couple to be happy. I was just glad to have the heat off me and Joaquin.

After the listening party I felt so inspired that I called Chauncey the next day to add a few more songs and today was the big release. We'd been on a media blitz and I was ready to fall asleep, but needed to get this done so I could take a vacation and finish getting the house together. Joaquin left for work at his office and said he would be here later for dinner. I already had a chef coming over tonight two hours early to prep, as well as a cleaning crew to make sure everything was just right. Cassidy followed along with me to New York for an interview with a local entertainment talk show about my music and new movie. Cassidy typed away on her phone as the makeup artist continued putting mascara on the fake eyelashes.

"Everything's all over social media about today's interview," Cassidy mentioned.

"I didn't expect anything less."

"Some are wondering if this album is about Joaquin," Cassidy spoke.

I shrugged, not giving an answer to the question. I had some songs about Joaquin, but not everything.

"Sofia we're ready for you," the talk show assistant said.

"Coming."

I passed my phone to Cassidy and headed to do my second interview for the day.

"You're looking lovely, Sofia," Brandy from *Entertainment Live* said.

I sat down across from her with my hands clasped together.

"Thank you."

"You have a glow about you," Brandy said.

"Probably my new album being out," I teased as I held it up for the camera.

"So, tell us what this album is about?" Brandy questioned.

"It's about my journey over the past few months and years."

"Would you say highs and lows?" Brandy inquired.

"Yes, the music video I did for "His Peace" is probably the rawest I've ever been."

"Your fans are wanting to know, are you in love?" Brandy asked.

"You know I like to keep my personal life private, but I will say I'm happy."

"The new movie looks great, are you planning more acting in the future?" Brandy asked.

"Hopefully, but I'm taking some time off after this press tour to spend time with my family."

"Thank you again for hanging with us, Sofia, I speak for all of your fans when I say we're glad you're back," Brandy spoke.

...

"Dad, I wanted to tell you something," Alessandra started to say.

"What is it?" I asked.

"Ummm..." Alessandra hesitated.

"Just spit it out," I said.

"Gael and I are dating!" Alessandra shouted.

He started to turn red and then glared at Gael.

"You knew about this?" he asked Joaquin.

"I learned about it recently and I'm happy she chose someone that I know could protect her the way she deserves to be protected," Joaquin mentioned.

"Mr. Fuertes, I love your daughter," Gael said.

"Alba, do you hear this?" Mr. Fuertes asked.

"I do and I'm happy to have both my children be in loving relationships," his mother stated.

"Father, I promise I'll finish school," Alessandra said.

"What about this Edward situation?" he asked and changed the subject.

"It's no longer an issue," Joaquin told her.

The detectives' bodies were found in a lake in the back of a trunk chopped up. It was all over the news that it was a mob hit; the timeline was poured over of when Jones and Adams were seen last. I remembered Joaquin saying he had to take care of some business one night, but I learned to stop asking questions. If Jones and Adams were smart they wouldn't have continued pressing me about Edward's disappearance. Alba asked for more wine and I smiled then poured more into her glass.

EPILOGUE

S*ofia*
Three years later.

I was riding in the back of a limo with Joaquin sitting beside me, holding my hand in a tight grip. Since the moment I was taken from him on the boat, he'd made it a priority to have me protected at all times even when I was working on set or recording my music. I tried to fight him, but he wouldn't listen and only told me for his own peace of mind that he needed me to be surrounded by people he could trust. Ever since then he has had a camera installed inside each vehicle that I used, plus a tracking device on the car and my ring. One night after dinner he slipped a ring out of his pocket and got down on one knee to propose. At first, I was shocked and it took me a few seconds to answer, but I knew I was in love and that I wanted to be with him no matter what. Here we were driving to an event that held the most dangerous people in the world. From what I gathered they held these events to talk business and introduce new players in the Cartel. I knew Sabrina and Janice were supposed to be there tonight and that made me feel better to know someone and not be hanging on every word that Joaquin said, as he introduced me as his fiancée. The gossip magazines had reported every other day that I was pregnant. One thing I could assure them of was that babies were not my biggest priority at the moment. Continuing my career and planning our wedding was the only thing I wanted, and I knew that Joaquin supports me. He can be reclusive, withdrawn, angry, and possessive at times. He was the man I loved, and I understood how his emotions got the better of him and trying to express them in a normal relationship with communication would be the ideal thing, but dating a mob boss came with bigger issues than a regular relationship.

"You ready, sweetheart?" Joaquin asked as he squeezed my hand as the car stopped in front of the Atlantis Hall in Queens. His driver came around to the right passenger side and opened the door for Joaquin and he stepped out, adjusted his coat, then held his hand out for me.

"Are you ready?"

"Long as you're by my side, I'll always be good," Joaquin replied before he leaned over to kiss my cheek.

The doors opened and we walked inside to a display of white linen draped around the room with high chandeliers in the middle. A small crowd gathered at the front as they went through security. I noticed they allowed us to pass through without being checked, and Joaquin nodded at the security guard. The tables were white and silver with lit candle centerpieces, and silver napkins looked to be engraved. A small band and stage with the De Luca name etched in gold was on the back wall.

"Why didn't they check us?" I questioned as I tugged on his arm.

"Antonio's people are behind the security for tonight," Joaquin responded as Carlo and Janice waved us over. I smiled and held my arms out for a hug and she extended her arms and we complimented each other on our dresses. I was wearing a gown by Carolina Herrera, a one-shoulder, draped, black mini dress.

"Let me see the ring," Janice asked, I held my hand out for her to see. "This is beautiful, Sofia," she responded and tapped Carlo on the shoulder as he talked to Joaquin.

"Carlo, do you see this ring?" Janice asked and Carlo nodded in answer.

"I do, babe," Carlo answered.

"Good, I expect to see something similar by tomorrow afternoon," Janice stated, and Carlo grinned before he pressed a kiss on her forehead.

"I can just imagine the conversations in your household," I said.

"Carlo thinks he's in control, but we both know who's the boss," Janice said as she looped her arm in mine and started to walk off. Joaquin gave me a look to stay close.

"She's fine, Joaquin. Everybody in here knows you'll blow the place up if something happens to her," Janice commented, and I chuckled knowing she was right.

"Where's Sabrina and Antonio?" I questioned as I looked around the room.

"At the front, right there. We can steal her away before it gets too boring," Janice mentioned.

"What should I expect from these gatherings?"

"Nothing but a bunch of men talking and the women gossiping," Janice stated.

Right as we approached Sabrina, she smiled, and Antonio glanced at who she was grinning at.

"Sofia, you look amazing. I need to borrow that dress," Sabrina told me, and hugged me with one arm.

"Same to you. I can't believe you have four kids and look this beautiful."

"I have no choice since I run after them all day, well the younger ones anyway," Sabrina said, grabbing a glass of champagne off the tray that passed through.

"How long do these meetings last?"

"About two or three hours, but we never stayed more than an hour," Sabrina answered, taking another sip of her drink.

I scanned the room, watched all the men laugh or whisper in conversation. It was interesting to see how Joaquin navigated in this world and he wanted me to be a part of it, at the same time to stay myself and not get jaded or scared.

"Who is that?" I heard Janice ask and point. I followed her stretched out arm and saw a young woman next to an older gentleman. She looked bored and ready to go like the rest of the women here.

"That's Gigi Carrington and her father, Laurent," Sabrina spoke.

"I thought he never brought his daughter anywhere because he was afraid she'd get harmed," Janice stated and Sabrina glared at Janice.

"It's fine, Sabrina, I'm past everything now," I said as I plastered on a smile.

"Did you seek therapy like I told you?" Sabrina inquired, and I responded with a curt nod.

"I'm glad to hear that, because I've been where you are, Sofia. Don't feel like you're alone," Sabrina said.

"Joaquin's been amazing and supportive. Plus, he asked me to be his wife so I doubt I could get away from him now." I laughed and waved my hand around.

"He's just like Antonio and Carlo. Once they get you, there's no way to escape their love," Sabrina mentioned, and we all agreed.

"What are you going to do about your career?" Janice asked.

"I have a new manager now, plus Cassidy is still working with me. I plan on keeping my career."

"What about kids?" Sabrina queried, as the men started to walk over to us.

"We're enjoying each other so hopefully one day we'll be blessed," I said.

"Ladies, I want to introduce you to someone," Antonio said as Joaquin came up behind me and wrapped his arm around my waist.

"This is Laurent Carrington and his daughter, Gigi," Antonio said, and Laurent reached out to shake our hands. For a moment, Gigi's eyes hung on the tall guy wearing all black who looked like he was security.

"Joaquin, you didn't mention how beautiful your fiancée is," Laurent said as he lifted my hand to plant a kiss.

"Laurent, you've been a married man for over forty years, don't cause that to end abruptly," Joaquin stated. I tilted my head and rolled my eyes at his comment. Anytime a guy flirted he had to threaten them in some way.

Laurent chuckled and cuffed Carlo's shoulder.

"It's nice to meet you, Laurent, and your daughter, Gigi."

"You too," Gigi responded in a soft, innocent voice.

The security guard's dark eyes shifted to Gigi and something about the longing in his eyes reminded me of Joaquin and I in the early beginning.

"Antonio, I heard your name was being brought up with the DEA and Interpol," Laurent blurted out and Sabrina twisted her wedding ring.

"Nothing I can't handle," Antonio remarked and shot

him a venomous look. I bet he didn't want Sabrina knowing what was going on.

"Ladies and gentlemen, it's time to take your seats for dinner," the announcer said.

Joaquin grasped my hand and we went to the first table that held seating cards that said De Luca and Fuertes. Joaquin pulled my chair out and I sat down with him beside me, the conversation turned to legit businesses starting up for Alba Industries. The waiters came out to each table with a lasagna, salmon, or chicken choice, plus a light salad to start. It felt like a coming out party for our relationship and no animosity or crazy enemies trying to break us apart anymore.

An hour later I was withering underneath Joaquin as he kissed up my stomach after we finished our second round of sex once we got home tonight. He laid back against the headboard and pulled me into his arms.

"Thank you," Joaquin muttered and I'd never heard him sound so relaxed and unsure in the same breath.

I looked up into his eyes and ran a hand across his chest.

"Why are you thanking me?"

"For not running when things got bad," Joaquin spoke and I grinned.

"You can't get rid of me that easily," I answered, pressed a kiss on his chest.

"I'd never want to, Sofia," Joaquin replied.

"Mr. Fuertes, do you love me?" I teased as I slid my hand underneath the covers.

He gasped as I slowly stroked his large girth back to life.

"Bellissima Sofia...You are my heart," Joaquin mumbled slowly.

"No matter good or bad...I won't run from you," I told

him, as we stared into each other's eyes. He smirked as I eased under the covers to give him the same special treatment that he descended on me tonight. I made a promise when I took his ring for better or worse, and we'd gone through the biggest hurdle and came above water together.

* * *

CHECK out **Joaquin and Sofia in book 3** here **Betrayed"** "https://books2read.com/u/4A5LGp .Follow my stand-alone opposites attract, age gap, military romance **"Exposed"** https://books2read.com/u/bQyYZe . Are you a fan of sports romance? Then download one-night stand, billionaire romance **"Refuel"** https://books2read.com/u/boDyDA. Also, follow it up with workplace, sports romance **"Pressure"** https://books2read.com/u/3Ly1r7 .If you love romantic comedy, fake relationships, enemies to lovers, find it here, **"Something Gained."** Click the link https://books2read.com/u/baGLYy .

Please also check out a second-chance, workplace romance here, **"Heart of Stone Book 4"** https://books2read.com/u/4NXyPG with a host of characters intertwined.

Follow Desiree and Gabriel in *"Temptation"* a stand-alone contemporary, sports, curvy girl romance. Check it out here https://books2read.com/u/mle1Vv

Check out mafia romance here, *"Antonio and Sabrina Book 1"* https://books2read.com/u/4AxKLo

Any fan of forbidden romance, political? Check out *"Mutual Agreement"* https://books2read.com/u/mgzzWX a steamy romance. Pre-order the full novel of **"Nasir"** here click the link here.

Have you checked out **"She's All I Need"** click here https://books2read.com/u/49lkeW a sports, opposites attract romance. What about dark romance that has everything from steamy romance, opposites attract, suspense, thriller, celebrity, and more "**Joaquin Fuertes Book 1**" https://books2read.com/u/mvZlgV

Catch up with favorite characters in this holiday short romance which includes spoilers. https://books2read.com/u/bzd59G

READING ORDER OF SERIES

Order of Reading
The Early Years-A Prequel Short Story
https://books2read.com/u/49Zjnw
Antonio and Sabrina Struck In Love Book 1
https://books2read.com/u/4AxKLo
Antonio and Sabrina Struck In Love Book 2
https://books2read.com/u/bpED6g
Antonio and Sabrina Struck In Love Book 3
https://books2read.com/u/3LpgdJ
Janice and Carlo Captivated By His Love
https://books2read.com/u/b6je6M
Antonio and Sabrina Struck In Love Book 4
https://books2read.com/u/4NQyE9
Joaquin Fuertes-The Fuertes Cartel Book 1
https://books2read.com/u/mvZlgV
Joaquin Fuertes-The Fuertes Cartel Book 2
https://books2read.com/u/4DWwLd
Antonio and Sabrina Struck In Love Book 5
https://books2read.com/u/b5kZ8O

Joaquin Fuertes-The Fuertes Cartel Book 3
https://books2read.com/u/4A5LGp

ORDER OF HEART OF STONE UNIVERSE

Heart of Stone Book 1 Emery and Jackson
https://books2read.com/u/boWPAV
Heart of Stone Book 1.5
https://books2read.com/u/mKELYZ
Heart of Stone Book 2 Jordan and Damon
https://books2read.com/u/ba2OMx
Heart of Stone Book 3.5 Bottoms Up
https://books2read.com/u/4EkjBg
Heart of Stone Book 3 Angela and Brent
https://books2read.com/u/31rx9l
Heart of Stone Book 4 Jessica and Joseph
https://books2read.com/u/4NXyPG

SNEAK PEEK - THE CARRINGTON CARTEL

Gigi's future has always been known. She's to marry into the Ramini family. Nothing matters more than that to her family.

As the daughter of the renowned Laurent Carrington, long-time gun and drug runner for the cartel, nothing about her life is ambiguous. She does what her father says or suffers the consequences.

Axel is good at his job. As lead enforcer for a notorious cartel associate, he's entrusted to monitor Gigi's every move. What he doesn't expect is to fall in love with her. Now he's faced with a tough choice—one that could cost him his life if he's not careful.

Will Gigi's plan to keep her arranged marriage at bay and keep her budding relationship with Axel sunder wraps shield her from her father's wrath, or will she go down an ugly path?

PLAYLIST

1.Monica-Without You

2.Missy Elliot -Hot Boyz

3.Jazmine Sullivan-Need U Bad

4.Rihanna-Love The Way You Lie

5.Jonas Bros-Sucker

6.India.Arie-Steady Love

7.Maroon Five-Girls Like You

8.Jason Mraz-Better With You

9.Thomas Rhett-Playing With Fire

10.Kendrick Lamar-Love

WHAT'S NEXT?

Want to know what happens next?

Follow me on my website to catch the next release.

Reviews are the lifeblood of the publishing world. They're read, appreciated, and needed.

Please consider taking the time to leave a few words on your review platform of choice.

Sign up for updates and sneak peaks at the site below.
www.chiquitadennie.com

ACKNOWLEDGMENTS

I want to dedicate this to my team that helps me behind the scenes, from my editors, test readers, graphic designers, and the list goes on. Truly appreciate each of you for keeping me on my toes.

CATALOGUE OF RELEASES

By Chiquita Dennie:
Temptation
The Early Years-A Prequel Short Story
Antonio & Sabrina: Struck in Love, Books 1, 2, 3,4
Janice & Carlo: Captivated by His Love
Heart of Stone, Book 1: Emery & Jackson
Heart of Stone, Book 1.5: Emery & Jackson, A Valentine's Day Short Story
Heart of Stone, Book 2: Jordan & Damon
Heart of Stone, Book 3: Angela & Brent
Heart of Stone, Book 3.5 Jessica & Joseph Bottoms Up
Joaquin Fuertes (The Fuertes Cartel Book 1)
Cocky Catcher (A Hero Club Novel)
Bossy Billionaire (A Hero Club Novel)
Love Shorts-A Collection of Short Stories

By KeKe Renée
His Peace Her Pleasure
Love Don't Live Here Anymore 1,2
Wet Heat

EveryTime We Touch (A Wet Heat Novelette)
One Night Only-A Novelette Book 1
Cassian and Savannah-Love By Design Book 2
Deidra's Love-Love By Design Book 3
Protecting Bria-Operation Alpha
Upcoming 2021
Haven

By Ava S. King
Agent Red-Fatal Memory (Teagan Stone Book 1)

Thank you so much for reading and if you enjoyed the crazy ride and decide to leave a review, we'd truly appreciate the support.

ABOUT THE AUTHOR

Chiquita Dennie is an emerging author of Contemporary, Romantic Suspense. Chiquita lives in Los Angeles, CA. Before she started writing contemporary romance, she worked in the entertainment industry on notable TV shows like Dr Phil show, the Tyra Banks show, American Idol, and Deal or No Deal. But her favorite job is the one she's now doing full time, writing romance.

She's a best-selling author and award-winning film-maker. Her first short film "Invisible" was released in the Summer 2017 and screened in multiple festivals and won for Best Short Film. Also, she hosts a podcast that show-cases the latest in Beauty, Business and Community called "Moscato and Tea." Her debut release of Antonio and Sabrina Struck In Love has opened a new avenue of writing that she loves.

If you want to know when the next book will come out, please visit my website at http://www.chiquitadennie.com, where you can sign up to receive an email for my next release.

304 PUBLISHING COMPANY

We showcase authors writing African American, Interracial, Women's Fiction, Urban Romance, Erotic, and Contemporary Romance novels. Along with Thriller, Suspense, Poetry, Beauty, and Style Books. Thank you for taking the time out to visit. Join our mailing list to stay updated with new releases and blog posts.

www.ingramcontent.com/pod-product-compliance
Lightning Source LLC
Chambersburg PA
CBHW011201190726
48286CB00009B/2875